W9-AZF-387

"I'm not really hungry."

"Are you sure? Please eat with me." He put on his best puppy-dog face and she laughed, then ordered a turkey sandwich with Swiss on wheat.

"Mayo, not mustard." They spoke the words aloud, in unison, and she turned, her face reflecting genuine surprise.

"You remembered."

"There are a lot of things I remember." *Like how beautiful you look in blue. How those brown eyes sparkle when you get mad. How you love working like a maniac to get the job done. How you get silly if you stay up too late.* Chris wanted to say more, but when Adrianne's cheeks flashed pink, he turned, instead, to place his order.

JANICE A. THOMPSON is a Christian author from Texas. She has four grown daughters, and the whole family is active in ministry, particularly the arts. Janice is a writer by trade but wears many other hats, as well. She previously taught drama and creative writing at a Christian school of the arts. She also directed a global drama missions team. She currently heads up the elementary department at her church and enjoys public speaking. Janice is passionate about her faith and does all she can to share it with others, which is why she particularly loves writing inspirational novels. Through her stories, she hopes to lead others into a relationship with a loving God.

Books by Janice A. Thompson

HEARTSONG PRESENTS

HP490—A Class of Her Own
HP593—Angel Incognito
HP613—A Chorus of One
HP666—Sweet Charity
HP667—Banking on Love
HP734—Larkspur Dreams—Coauthored with Anita Higman

Don't miss out on any of our super romances. Write to us at the following address for information on our newest releases and club information.

Heartsong Presents Readers' Service
PO Box 721
Uhrichsville, OH 44683

Or visit www.heartsongpresents.com

Red Like Crimson

Janice A. Thompson

Heartsong Presents

To Michelle and baby Jacob. . .welcome home.

A note from the Author:
I love to hear from my readers! You may correspond with me by writing:

Janice A. Thompson
Author Relations
PO Box 721
Uhrichsville, OH 44683

ISBN 978-1-59789-592-7

RED LIKE CRIMSON

Copyright © 2007 by Janice A. Thompson. All rights reserved. Except for use in any review, the reproduction or utilization of this work in whole or in part in any form by any electronic, mechanical, or other means, now known or hereafter invented, is forbidden without the permission of Heartsong Presents, an imprint of Barbour Publishing, Inc., PO Box 721, Uhrichsville, Ohio 44683.

All scripture quotations, unless otherwise indicated, are taken from the New King James Version®. Copyright © 1982 by Thomas Nelson, Inc. Used by permission. All rights reserved.

Scripture quotations marked KJV are taken from the King James Version of the Bible.

All of the characters and events in this book are fictitious. Any resemblance to actual persons, living or dead, or to actual events is purely coincidental.

Our mission is to publish and distribute inspirational products offering exceptional value and biblical encouragement to the masses.

PRINTED IN THE U.S.A.

prologue

Virginia Beach

The small linen envelope contained a simple "Dear John" letter. Nothing more. So why did Adrianne's hands tremble as she slipped it underneath the door? Why did she struggle to press down the accompanying lump in her throat?

Surely in her three years at the university, she'd faced tougher writing assignments than this brief, handwritten note. Last week's philosophy paper, for example. And the term paper for her Humanities class last spring. Yes, she had certainly completed lengthier projects. But never one more personal.

Adrianne stood and brushed her palms against her jeans, as if by doing so she could wash this whole, ugly thing from her memory before turning and walking away.

And yet it hadn't all been ugly, had it? She allowed her mind to visit the hidden places as she eased away from the door. No, most parts of it had been wonderful. Completely wonderful. Even pure. But somewhere along the way, things had taken an ugly turn, and reality had come around full circle.

Now she must face facts, though facing them surely meant releasing every dream she'd ever held tucked away in the recesses of her heart. She couldn't stay. Not one day more, in fact, even if it meant leaving college in the middle of the semester.

As Adrianne inched her way along the corridor, she tried to avoid the eyes of fellow students passing by. Many laughed and talked together. Their voices layered on top of each other, creating a cacophony of sounds, much like a symphony coming into tune. Such chaos among the students she had grown to expect, even appreciate. But one voice she could not squelch.

"Come now, and let us reason together. . . ."

The all too familiar words from the Bible she had loved since childhood rose to the surface again, and the lump in her throat became unbearable.

"I've spent all morning reasoning," she whispered to the skies. "I've tried to be logical. But, Lord, surely You can see this is the only way."

"Though your sins are like scarlet. . ."

A cool breeze whipped through the courtyard outside the dormitory, not unusual for early autumn in Virginia Beach. The leaves, in varying shades of red and gold, rippled through tree branches overhead, as if begging to be released. She understood their pain.

At that moment, a light breeze caused many to tumble down in colorful array. A sign, perhaps, that moving on— letting go—was the better choice?

"Oh, Lord. I'm so sorry. So very, very sorry." She closed her eyes and whispered a good-bye to Virginia Beach. In just a few short hours she would return home—to Philadelphia. For good. There, much like those fallen leaves, she would face the cold, hard reality of winter, and would surely come to terms with the consequences of her sins.

"Though they are red like crimson. . ."

Adrianne stopped walking and stood a moment in silence— wanting to look back, and yet knowing she could only move forward.

If only her heart would move forward with her.

one

Philadelphia, eight years later

Adrianne rushed around the apartment in a tizzy. "Have you seen my shoe?" she called out. "I'm missing my right shoe!"

Her daughter appeared at the bedroom door with a comical look on her face. The vivacious seven-year-old dangled a dainty black pump from her fingertip. "You lose *everything*, Mom." She rolled her eyes, but Adrianne noticed a twinkle there.

"I know, I know." Adrianne pushed aside the wispy strands of her daughter's light brown hair as she reached to plant a kiss on her forehead. "You're the mother and I'm the daughter. Right?"

"No way!" Lorelei's face erupted in a smile and her green eyes danced with mischief. "I want to be the kid. I don't want to have to go to work." She passed off the shoe, then sprang onto the bed.

Adrianne gazed into her daughter's face with the most serious expression she could muster. "School is better then?"

Lorelei nodded, eyes widening. "Indubitably."

"Indubitably?" Adrianne repeated the word, to make sure she'd heard it correctly. "Since when do you use words like *indubitably*?"

"Grandma says it all the time."

And you're using it in context. Not bad for a seven-year-old.

Adrianne hopped up and down in an attempt to get the wayward shoe into place. Once she had it secured on her foot,

7

she glanced up at the mirror above the oak dresser. "Oh, my hair. It looks awful." She attempted to press the dark curls into place with her fingertips, but, as always, her unruly hair had a mind of its own and would not cooperate.

Before another word could be spoken, Lorelei bounded from the bed and handed her the hairbrush. "Your hair is *so* pretty, Mom." The little darling let out an exaggerated sigh, one Adrianne had grown to anticipate during such mother-daughter conversations. "I wish my hair was pretty like yours."

Lorelei joined her at the mirror, mother and daughter now standing side-by-side, staring at the glass. "Better be careful what you wish for." Adrianne spoke to her daughter's reflection as she pulled the brush through her wayward curls. "I used to wish for a little girl. And look what I got. . . ."

"The best kid in the world!" Lorelei hollered out.

"Puh-leeze!" Tossing the brush aside, Adrianne reached over to tickle her precocious daughter, and they both broke into raucous laughter. Seconds later, the neighbor from the apartment next door banged on the wall.

"Enough, already!" Mr. Sanderson hollered out, his voice somewhat muffled through the thin layer of sheetrock. "I'm trying to sleep over here. Don't you people ever stop?"

With a finger to her lips, Adrianne led her daughter from the room, tiptoeing all the way. They gathered up their belongings and headed out of the apartment to face the day.

Moments later, they stood at the bus stop together, waiting for the school bus to arrive. In the field to her right, the first fall leaves had tumbled to the ground. Adrianne closed her eyes a moment, remembering another autumn, years ago. *"Though your sins are like scarlet. . ."*

"Mom, I'm c–cold." Lorelei spoke through chattering teeth.

Adrianne snapped to attention and buttoned her daughter's jacket, then wrapped her in a warm embrace. "Is that better?"

"Mm-hmm."

At this point, Adrianne released her hold, opting for a game of distraction, one they often played together on mornings like this. "Name five great things about living in Philadelphia," she coached.

"That's easy." Lorelei giggled. "Philly cheese steak."

"Philly cheese steak tops your list?"

"Mm-hmm. And the Liberty Bell."

"Good girl. What else?"

The youngster's nose wrinkled. "Grandma and Grandpa."

"Naturally. Although, your grandmother will be devastated to learn she's so far down on the list. What else? Or should I say *who* else. . . ?"

"You."

"I was beginning to wonder if you'd forgotten about me." Adrianne glanced at her watch. *7:34? If that bus doesn't come soon, I'm going to be late for work.* "Name one more thing."

A pensive look crossed the youngster's face, followed by a shrug. "I don't know, Mom. I can't think of anything else."

"Excuse me?" Adrianne crossed her arms and presented her most serious face. "You can't think of anything else about living in Philadelphia, Pennsylvania—the very birthplace of freedom?"

Lorelei shrugged.

"Let me see if I can refresh your memory then." Adrianne slipped into teacher mode. "One of our country's founding fathers once lived in this very spot." She pressed a hand to her heart, feeling the swell of patriotism.

"Mom, puh-leeze!"

Undeterred, Adrianne carried on. "He was a printer, a postmaster, and an inventor. Some claim that he discovered electricity by flying a kite in a storm. He signed both the Declaration of Independence and the Constitution of the

United States." Here, Adrianne's shoulders rose in pride. Her voice intensified as she finished. "And your mother currently works as a curator at the museum named in his honor."

"I know, I know." Lorelei's eyes narrowed as she gave the matter some thought. "The Ben Franklin Museum."

"The Franklin Institute, to be precise," Adrianne admonished.

Lorelei groaned, clearly tired of this part of the game. "You tell me all the time."

"And I'll go on telling you, too. Until you remember every detail."

At that very moment, the bus arrived. Adrianne reached to give her daughter a peck on the cheek, then the youngster climbed aboard en route to school.

Not one minute too soon. With no time to spare, Adrianne settled into her car and headed downtown. As she drew close to the familiar museum, excitement grew. She had adored this place since childhood. She loved the artifacts, the paintings, and the clothing displays. She loved the hustle and bustle of tourists as they made the rounds from one venue to the next, oohing and aahing over all of the wonderful things the facility had to offer.

More than anything, she hoped to instill this same love for America's rich history into her daughter. Whether the little monster wanted it or not.

"Girl, you're late!" Dani Jennings looked up from her paperwork with a scolding smile as Adrianne entered the museum lobby.

"I know, I know. Lorelei's bus was late. Again."

Her petite coworker shrugged. "At least you don't have to worry about Mr. Martinson chewing you out. He thinks you hung the moon."

"Hardly."

"One of these days he will retire and you'll be senior curator.

Wait and see." Dani winked.

Adrianne tried to suppress a smile. Perhaps one day soon she would work her way up the ladder. For now, she was plenty happy to carry on as an associate. Thrilled, in fact.

"What does the morning look like?" Adrianne stepped behind the counter and noticed a stack of papers.

"Quite a few tour groups, but Joey is here. So's Brenna. A school bus just pulled up with fifty third-graders."

"Saw that." Adrianne shuffled through the papers on the top of the stack, noting several RSVPs for the upcoming fundraising banquet.

Dani continued on, oblivious. "We've got a private group coming in at ten thirty. A wedding party. They'll be lunching at the bistro afterward. They've already placed their order."

"Ah. Okay." What was it, though, about the words *wedding party* that brought a sigh to Adrianne's lips?

"For the life of me," Dani went on, "I don't understand all of these wedding groups coming through. As much as I love this place, I can't imagine bringing my bridesmaids to a museum as a form of pre-wedding entertainment. I can think of a thousand other places I'd take them, but. . .a museum?"

Adrianne offered up a shrug. "Oh, I don't know. It's something fun to do together." And why not? Usually, the bride or groom hailed from the Philadelphia area and simply wanted to show off the historic aspects of the city he or she loved. Nothing wrong with that.

"I'm just saying that if I had a life outside of the things of the past"—Dani gestured to the inner sanctum of the museum—"I'd stick to the present. Especially on the week of my wedding."

"If I had a life outside of the past. . ."

Dani turned her attention to the school group. Adrianne shrugged off her friend's words and headed to her office, where she dove into her paperwork with a vengeance. She would sooner do anything than focus on the past, today of all days.

To Adrianne's amazement, the morning flew by. She spent a little time looking over plans to update the Wright Brothers display, and then telephoned the professional party planner she'd hired to take care of the upcoming fundraising banquet.

In the midst of that conversation, Dani appeared at her office door, breathless. "Adrianne, I hate to interrupt, but this is important."

Adrianne looked up from the phone and, with a raised index finger, whispered, "Just a minute." She finished the call, then turned to face Dani head-on. "What's up?"

Her friend's pretty blue eyes sparkled and the pitch of her voice rose as she shared her news. "Mr. Kenner is here to talk to you about the consultation grant."

"Ooh!" Adrianne gasped. "You're kidding. I didn't expect him till next week."

"I know. But he says you're going to want to talk to him now." Dani's face broadened in a smile. "Sounds like good news."

Adrianne felt her heart rate quicken. Perhaps her most recent prayers for the museum had truly been answered. "I sure hope you're right." She fumbled with her purse, reaching for the tube of lipstick. "I'll be there in just a minute."

She pulled open a compact and dabbed on the rosy-colored lipstick, then sprinted in the direction of the meeting room at the back of the museum. As she rounded the corner just beyond the electricity display, she ran headlong into Joey, who happened to be leading the bridal party tour.

"I'm so sorry." She offered up a shrug. "Going too fast for my own good."

"Not a problem." Joey flashed a broad smile and gestured to the group, his spiked blond hair standing at attention. "But let me introduce you to these fine people."

Adrianne drew in a breath, a little frustrated at the interruption. What should she do about Mr. Kenner, who waited in the meeting room? For weeks, she'd awaited news from him, and now he waited on her. She didn't want to keep him long, not with so much at stake.

"Ladies and gentlemen," Joey spoke with flair, "I'd like to introduce one of our most admired curators, Adrianne Russo. She's been with the museum for four years, and has made improvements to several of our displays, including the one you're viewing right now."

She took note of the words *most admired* with a sigh, and then looked across the group of people with a rehearsed smile. Which one was the bride? *Ah. The one with the glow on her face.* And the groom must be the one to her right with his arm around her waist. A cluster of lovely bridesmaids stood nearby and. . .

She glanced to her left to take in the group of groomsmen. Her gaze ran from one young man to the next, finally landing on the taller one at the end of the line.

As their eyes met, Adrianne's heart flew into her throat. For a moment, she could scarcely catch her breath. *No! Not here. Not like this.*

From just a few short yards away, the man she had once loved more than life itself stared back in stunned silence. And in that moment, eight years of unspoken words traveled between them.

two

Christopher stared at Adrianne in disbelief. Except for the length of her dark brown curls and the uncharacteristic professional attire, she looked every bit as she had the day he'd seen her last.

Virginia Beach. Eight years ago. Eight years of questioning, wondering, worrying. Eight years of trying to figure out if his actions had driven her to leave town, with no notice other than a note under his door.

"I—I. . ." Adrianne's face paled and she turned away from the group and sprinted down the hallway. Christopher pulled away from the rest of his group and followed after her, unable to still the hammering of his heart.

Still running? Why, Adrianne? Why?

On she raced, a woman on a mission.

"Adrianne, wait." When she didn't slow, he called out, "Please!"

She came to a halt, then slowly turned to face him, her eyes filled with tears. "I'm sorry, Chris. I—I can't talk right now."

Can't or won't?

"I have a meeting." She shot a glance at her wristwatch and looked back up with a pained expression. "I'm sorry, but I don't have any choice."

"Well, then, I'm going to wait for you," he managed, pushing aside the lump in his throat. When she started to argue, he added, "I don't care how long it takes. I've waited eight years. I can wait a little longer."

She drew in a deep breath and nodded. Then, without a word, she disappeared into a door on the right.

Chris leaned against the wall to collect his thoughts. *Why now, Lord? After all this time? After all of my unanswered letters?*

At that moment, his best friend, Stephen, appeared at his side, a look of intrigue on his face. "Something you want to tell me, man?"

"Um, I. . ."

Stephen shrugged. "She's a knockout, but she doesn't look familiar to any of us."

She wouldn't.

"Doesn't resemble you, so she's definitely not your sister. A long-lost cousin, maybe?"

"No. Not my sister or my cousin." *Almost my wife.* Chris slid down the wall and sat on the floor.

Stephen looked down at him, clearly intrigued. "Interesting game we're playing," he observed. "Wish I knew how it was going to come out in the end."

"You and me both." Chris closed his eyes and tried to make sense of all this. How could he begin to explain? When Adrianne had bolted from his life years ago, the hole in his heart had been huge. For months, he had grieved both the loss of her love and her friendship.

And her respect.

His breaths grew faster as he thought about it now. How many letters had he sent to her parents' home in Philly those first two years? Fifteen? Twenty? And how many times had she responded?

None.

"When you're ready to talk, I'm here." Stephen crossed his arms and cast a pensive gaze his way.

"When you're ready to talk. . ." Chris's mind flashed back to a phone message he'd left for Adrianne nearly eight years prior. He had spoken those same words. *"When you're ready to talk, Adrianne, I'm here."* Apparently she hadn't been ready then.

And judging from the look on her face, she wasn't ready now, either. In his heart, he suspected the reason for her leaving. He had blamed himself all these years—and rightfully so.

"I tried to tell her I was sorry." He spoke the words aloud now and brushed the mist from his eyes.

Stephen stared down at him, a concerned look registering on his face. "Sorry for what?"

"We dated for nearly two years," Chris whispered. "And I promised her—promised God—that we wouldn't. . ."

"Wouldn't what?" Stephen sat on the floor next to him.

Chris sighed. "We were going to wait until we got married. We promised each other. I'm not sure when things started to slip, but they did. I take full responsibility. I should have stopped it, should have. . ."

"Chris, it happens to the best of us," Stephen said with a look of understanding in his eyes. "We all make mistakes."

"But we were in Bible college. I was going into the ministry. Missions, no less. If anyone needed to stay pure. . ."

"Chris, God calls all of us to live in purity," Stephen said. "Being in the ministry doesn't make you more accountable. But it does make you more vulnerable, at least to some extent."

"I disagree." Chris shook his head. "Being in the ministry *does* make me more accountable. And I take full responsibility. I'm completely to blame here. No doubt about that. Somewhere along the way I. . .we. . .crossed a line. And I lost her because of it. She left."

"Left?"

"The school. The relationship. Everything. Just. . .left." Chris closed his eyes and thought back to the note she'd left under his door. "Adrianne said we couldn't turn back the clock, couldn't go back to the way things were before. She said she had to"—he swallowed hard—"had to get her life back on track. When I read her letter, I just broke. My mistakes cost me the one person I loved above all others."

"Look"—Stephen reached over to give him a squeeze on the shoulder—"I don't claim to have the answers. But I know you, and I know you're a good man. A godly man. I'm sure you've made mistakes along the way. We all have."

Chris looked up, hope setting in, and whispered, "Thanks."

"You've already made things right with the Lord. And it's not too late to ask for Adrianne's forgiveness." Stephen stood and offered him a hand up. "Maybe that's why God has led you here."

"Maybe." Chris contemplated the possibility. *Lord, are You behind all of this?*

"I don't believe in coincidence."

"Me, neither." Chris stood alongside his friend and sighed. "And I thought I was in Philly to be your best man."

"Always a groomsman, never a groom." Stephen chuckled.

Chris groaned. "I know. Don't remind me." How many times had he played this role through the years? Four? Five?

"Your day is coming." Stephen patted him on the back. "But in the meantime, it looks like the Lord has given you an opportunity to get some things off your chest."

Chris nodded, unable to speak.

"I'll be praying for you, my friend." Stephen glanced down the hallway. "But right now I'd better get back to my bride-to-be. I'm surprised she hasn't come looking for me yet. And you. . ." He gestured Chris's way. "When you're done meeting with Adrianne, join us in the restaurant, okay?"

"Okay."

Stephen headed off down the hallway, turning as he reached the end. "By the way," he called back, "that 'always a groomsman' remark was just a joke!"

Chris forced a smile. "Yeah, I know. Don't worry about it."

For now, he would happily play that role. Perhaps, one day, the Lord would shift him into another.

three

Adrianne tried to focus on Mr. Kenner, tried to stay tuned in to the excitement in his voice as he told her about the incoming grant money. On any other day, she would have jumped for joy. But today, with Chris on the other side of the door, her thoughts volleyed between joy, intrigue, and sheer terror.

"Are you okay, Miss Russo?" Mr. Kenner reached to pat her arm, a look of concern on his face.

Adrianne nodded in silence.

He chuckled, then broke into a broad smile. "I can tell you're in shock. I understand. It's a huge amount of money. I'm sure it's going to take awhile to sink in."

Another nod.

"I'll be in touch within a day or so to fill you in on the details," he added. "In the meantime, feel free to share the news with your employees. Looks like we'll have a lot to celebrate at the fundraising extravaganza."

Adrianne snapped to attention and extended her hand. "Mr. Kenner, I can never thank you enough." Tears erupted, but she didn't even try to force them down. "That grant money means the world to us." She managed a smile as he gripped her hand.

"I've told you"—he made direct eye contact and gave her hand a gentle squeeze—"to call me James."

"James." She stared into the man's eyes about three or four seconds, just long enough to grasp his all-too-personal meaning. At that point, she withdrew her hand from his and returned to a more businesslike stance. "I'll look forward to your call."

"And I, as well." He offered another pat on the arm as he

turned to leave the room. Her gaze followed the handsome thirty-something as he left, but her mind never shifted from another man—the one standing outside the door.

Christopher Bradley. The love of her life. The one who still took her breath away, still drained every ounce of normalcy from her at the very sight of him.

And he hadn't lost a bit of his charm or his shocking good looks.

Adrianne closed her eyes a moment and tried to collect her wits before walking out into that hallway to face him head-on. For some reason, her thoughts gravitated to his beautiful green eyes. How they had once swayed her with their love.

But no more. No, she was a grown woman now, a woman capable of looking forward, not behind. What was it Dani had said? Ah yes. *"If I had a life outside of the things of the past, I'd stick to the present."*

"Thank You, Lord, that I'm not ruled by my past," Adrianne now whispered. Certainly there were many issues to dredge up, if she cared to do so. But all of the mistakes of yesterday had been washed clean away, dealt with once and for all.

Hadn't they?

A little shiver ran down her spine and she offered up one last prayer before leaving the room. "Father, not my will but Yours be done." And then, with a resolute spirit, she tiptoed out into the hallway to see if Chris had, indeed, waited for her, as he'd promised.

Yes. She couldn't help but smile as their eyes locked. He'd waited. And the look on his face told her he would have stayed till midnight, if necessary.

"Adrianne. . ." His eyes misted over and he reached to take her hand. It wrapped hers perfectly, like a glove. Nothing had changed there.

"Chris." She gestured for him to join her in the meeting

room, and he followed like a puppy on her heels as she ushered him inside. Adrianne closed the door behind them, then offered him a chair.

Once seated, Adrianne drew her hands into her lap and clasped them together. A protective habit, really. Even after all of this time, she still inwardly longed for the feel of his hand in hers. Nothing could ever replace that.

"I'm sure you have a thousand questions," she began.

"Probably more than that." He offered up a weak smile. "But I only want you to say what you're comfortable saying."

Only what you're comfortable saying. . . How could she say anything at all, since the very things to tumble forth would surely reveal years of untold truths?

Adrianne took a deep breath and pushed back the tears that threatened to erupt. *Lord, I sense Your timing here. I don't want to blow this.* She gazed into Chris's beautiful eyes and began.

"Leaving you was the hardest thing I've ever done in my life. I need you to know that."

His eyes misted over right away and he nodded a bit before speaking. "*Losing* you was the hardest thing I've ever been through."

She instinctively glanced down at his left hand, in search of a ring. Surely, after all these years, Chris had married, started a family. Surely, he wouldn't still be single.

Nope. No ring.

For whatever reason, a wave of joy washed over her. She fought to suppress it.

"Before you go on," Chris said, interrupting her thoughts, "there's something I have to say to you. I've waited a long time to say it, but I can't let it go any longer. I know the Lord has brought me all the way from Nicaragua to Pennsylvania to speak these words. I'm. . .amazed. Grateful. But I'm terrified."

"Terrified?" She was the one who owed him an explanation,

not the other way around.

Chris placed his hand on her arm as he spoke. "Adrianne, you were the love of my life. And I wanted to treat you with the respect and dignity every woman deserves. I wanted to marry you, to make you my wife."

A lump grew in Adrianne's throat and her gaze shifted to her hands as he continued.

"I'm so ashamed," he said. "I let my physical desires get in the way of what God wanted. I took advantage of the situation, and I took advantage of you." He reached to lift her chin so that they were now eye to eye. "And in doing so destroyed any hope of a relationship with the one person I loved above everyone else on the planet."

Her heart felt as if it had been pressed upward from her chest into her throat.

"I don't blame you for leaving," he continued. "You were right to leave."

"Oh, Chris. . ." *If only you knew. . .*

"I read your letter a hundred times. And the things you said were right. We couldn't have turned back the clock, couldn't have gone back to the way things were before. My mind-set was so wrong back then. I tried to justify everything. Told myself we were going to get married. Told myself you were already mine. . ."

I told myself those same things.

"I need to ask your forgiveness," he whispered. "I've wanted— needed to do this for eight years."

"You weren't the only one who messed up," she said. Whether she wanted to voice it or not, Chris hadn't taken advantage of her. She could have drawn a line in their relationship. But she had willingly participated. Willingly. And doing so had changed not just her relationship with him, but everything.

"Losing you nearly killed me," he went on. "And I want you

to know—I *need* you to know—that I really tried to reach you. Multiple times, in fact. I sent letters. A couple dozen."

"I know." Tears began right away. "I read them."

"You did?" His face lit with joy. "You read them?" She nodded and he reached to squeeze her hands. "Adrianne, why didn't you let me know that you were okay? I knew the relationship was beyond repair, but I was so worried about you."

She shook her head and brushed aside the tears. "I—I . . . It's complicated. I was so scared."

"Scared of what?" He gazed into her eyes, begging for answers.

And he deserved them, didn't he? Hadn't he gone for eight long years without knowing the truth? How could she go on keeping it from him now? "Chris. . . ," she began. "There's something I need to tell you. But I don't think this is the right time, and I know for a fact it isn't the right place." She quickly jotted down her cell phone number on a scrap of paper and handed it to him. "Let's plan to meet while you're in town."

"C–can we get together this weekend?" He fingered the tiny piece of paper, clearly nervous. "I'm only going to be here for the next few days for my friend's wedding."

"Still playing the role of best man?" she asked with a smile.

He shrugged. "Yeah. But please don't say it. I hear it all the time from everyone else."

She wouldn't say it. She wouldn't dare.

No, if she spoke anything at all, it would be the story that began eight long years ago—the story that would change his life forever.

&

Chris walked toward the bistro, deep in thought. As he and Adrianne had arranged to meet the following day, he couldn't shake the feeling that she had something specific on her mind, something she might have shared today, if circumstances had been better. She had stopped short of telling him something of major importance. He sensed it to the core of his being.

Lord, I feel like I'm shooting in the dark here. But I know You see everything. Help me see it all in Your time.

Chris continued on down the hallway alone, reflecting on everything that had just transpired. What a miracle to stumble across Adrianne after all these years. Seeing her had sent his heavy heart into flight. Her lyrical voice. The way the end of her nose tipped up. The light in her rich doe-colored eyes when she spoke. Nothing had changed.

And yet, with the very next breath he had to conclude the obvious. . . .

Everything had changed.

four

"Where's that girl of mine?" Adrianne entered the familiar spacious living room at her parents' house, but couldn't find a soul. "Hello?" She wound her way into the kitchen, which was still decorated in shades of the 1980s. Country blue wallpaper lined each wall, and her mother's now infamous collection of ducks abounded. Adrianne couldn't help but chuckle as she remembered her mother's enthusiasm over "all things country." The fad had ended in most homes by the '90s, but not in her mother's kitchen, oh no.

"Hello?" Adrianne called again.

Nothing. No one.

"Hello?" She tried one more time.

Through the sliding glass door at the back of the house, she saw wisps of smoke rising into the early evening sky. *Ah. Dad's barbecuing again.* She opened the door and peeked outside, a delicious smell greeting her.

"Hey there!" she called out.

"Mom!" Lorelei squealed and ran her way. The youngster wrapped herself around Adrianne's waist, as always, bouncing up and down all the while. "You're home!"

Funny, how her daughter still referred to her grandma and grandpa's house as home, even after years of living in their own apartment.

"Were you good for your grandpa?" Adrianne asked.

"Gooder'n gold." Adrianne's dad turned from the barbecue grill long enough to respond. "But then again, she always is. That girl's the apple of her grandpa's eye."

"I know, I know." Adrianne sighed. "She can do no wrong." *Little monster. She can get away with anything where her grandparents are concerned.*

"Grandma, Mom's here!" Lorelei's lyrical voice rang out, and Adrianne turned to see her mother coming out of the back door with a tray of corn on the cob in her hands.

"I heard you come through," her mother said with a smile. "But I was on the phone in the bedroom. One of the ladies at church is in the middle of a crisis, and you know I'm the one who heads up the prayer chain."

"Yes. Of course."

"Anyway, I'm glad you're here," her mother added. "You're just in time for dinner."

"Mom, you don't have to feed us. I'm perfectly capable of. . ." She wanted to say she was perfectly capable of caring for the needs of her daughter on her own, but that would be wrong. Adrianne's parents thrived on helping out with Lorelei. And Adrianne thrived on letting them.

"Help me out with this, would you, honey?" Her mother passed off the tray. "I need to get back inside to work on that cheesecake we're having for dessert."

"Mmm. Yummy!" Lorelei clapped her hands. "I love cheesecake." The youngster bounded off into the house with her grandmother and Adrianne approached her father at the grill.

"More food here for you to cook." She nodded as she set down the tray.

He opened the top of the grill and pushed aside large, juicy pieces of chicken to make room for the corn on the cob. "If you think this looks like a feast, you should see the baked beans your mother's made. And the salad. You'd think she was feeding an army."

"What's the special occasion?"

"Ah. You've forgotten then?"

Adrianne racked her brain, trying to remember. *Not their anniversary. No one's birthday.* "What?"

"Today marks the eight-year anniversary of the day you came back to Philly to be with us." He gave her an endearing look.

"Ah. Yes, you're right." Funny, since this morning she'd completely forgotten.

"Seems like just yesterday."

"Not to me." An exaggerated sigh escaped her lips. "Seems like a lifetime ago." She pulled her jacket a bit tighter, fighting off the evening chill.

"I remember the look on your face the night you sat me down to tell me you were expecting Lorelei." Tears filled her father's eyes as he spoke.

"Oh, Dad. I'm so sorry. I'm *still* sorry for hurting you and Mom."

He shook his head. "I'll admit it was a hard pill to swallow. Your relationship with the Lord had always been so strong, and I knew your convictions were, too. And I could see how disappointed you were in yourself. I guess that's why I responded like I did."

He'd responded with all the love of a father aching for his baby girl to be made whole again.

"You showed me love when I didn't deserve it," Adrianne whispered.

He dabbed at his eyes with the back of his hand. "How many times has God done that for me? He would ask me to do no less for you."

"Dad"—Adrianne pushed back the lump in her throat, grateful for his response—"I need to talk to you about something. I need your advice." A little shiver worked its way up her spine as she mustered up the courage to forge ahead.

"You do?" His lips curled up in a pleasurable grin. "It makes the old man feel good to know his little girl still needs him. What kind of advice are we talking here? Something to do with the museum?"

"No. Nothing that easy." She waited a moment, then finally the words came. "Chris is in town."

Her father immediately lifted his spatula from the grill and turned with a pensive stare. "Are you sure?"

Adrianne nodded. "He showed up at the museum today."

"Looking for you?" The spatula trembled in his hand and he set it down on the side of the grill.

"No. He's in town for a wedding."

"Still playing the best man, or. . ." Her father paused. "Is this *his* wedding?"

Adrianne tried to gauge her father's expression. "Best man. But he didn't come looking for me. We just stumbled across one another at the museum—a coincidence."

"Hmm. Doesn't sound like one to me." He shook his head, albeit slowly. "More like a God-incidence, maybe?"

"Maybe." She offered up a shrug.

They both stood in silence for a while. Adrianne knew what her father must be thinking. He finally cut through the stillness with the question she knew he would ask.

"Does he know?"

"No." She whispered the word as if afraid the evening wind might pick it up and carry it off across the city to wherever Chris was. "He has no idea."

Her father's brow wrinkled. "Don't you think it's time, honey? I mean, don't you think God has arranged all of this? I'm sure you're nervous, but. . ."

"I've always wanted him to know he has a daughter." Adrianne pulled up a seat and leaned forward with her elbows on her knees. "I mean, I struggled with telling him when I was pregnant. And I let the months go by when I probably should have said something right away, especially in light of all the letters he sent that first year. But I was so worried about him pulling away from the ministry. . . ."

"I remember."

"When Lorelei was an infant, I called the school to see if anyone knew where he'd gone. I was told he was on the mission field in Nicaragua." Her heart twisted as she remembered the regret she'd felt that day. And yet, in the same breath, a certain amount of excitement had registered, too. How many times had he shared his dream of reaching out to the people of Central America with the gospel message? And how many times had she hung on his every word, like a starry-eyed schoolgirl?

Her father's face registered his shock at this news. "Why didn't you tell us? We always thought you didn't want him to know."

Adrianne pondered his words. She had been terrified. At the time. But keeping the truth from him just felt wrong.

"I tracked down the name of the mission organization," she explained. "And when I found it, they told me he was out in the field, training the locals to dig water wells—hours outside of Managua." She still remembered the swell of pride she'd felt upon receiving that news. "He was doing what he'd always dreamed of doing," her voice drifted off. "And I didn't want to take that from him. Besides, they said he couldn't be reached unless it was an emergency."

"And you didn't think it was?" Her father closed the grill and gazed into her eyes with compassion.

"I—I don't know. At least, I didn't at the time." Her next words were rushed. "I wanted to tell him, I really did. That's why I tried so hard to find him. But relaying a message through someone else. . . I don't know. It just felt wrong."

"Well, it looks like he has found you."

"Yes."

At that moment, the back door opened and Lorelei bounded out, her voice rising in glee. "Grandma bought me a present!" she squealed. She held up a DVD case with one of her favorite new movies inside.

Adrianne shook her head. "Good grief. It's not your birthday."

Her mother appeared at the door. "I know that." She shrugged. "But in a way, today is like a birthday for us. This is the day we got our daughter back. And it's the day we found out about little birdie-bye here." She ran her fingers through Lorelei's soft curls.

Silence permeated the backyard for a moment as that thought sank in. Eight years ago tonight, Adrianne had stood on this very porch and spilled her story to heartbroken parents. Amazing, how far they'd all come.

"So, what were you and Daddy talking about out here?" her mother asked, as she placed pieces of chicken from the grill onto a large serving plate.

"Oh. . ." Adrianne glanced at her daughter, knowing better than to delve into this with Lorelei looking on. "We were talking about—"

"The past," her father interrupted. "And the future."

"Oh?" Her mother's eyebrows arched. "Something specific going on I need to know about, or is this father-daughter stuff?"

It's father-daughter stuff, all right. Adrianne looked down into Lorelei's sparkling eyes—eyes that mimicked her daddy's in full—and struggled to contain her emotion. How much more specific could you get than the life of a child?

"I have some things to tell you, Mom," she whispered on the sly. "But not right now. Right now"—she raised her voice—"right now, I feel like eating."

And with that, they turned their attention to the celebration dinner.

five

The following day, Chris managed to slip away from his friends for a couple of hours to visit with Adrianne. He had tossed and turned in the uncomfortable hotel room bed for the better part of the night, trying to decide exactly what he would say when he had the opportunity. Nothing could stop him now.

He tracked down Adrianne at the museum, in the Wright Brothers display. She didn't see him coming, so he spent a moment or two analyzing her as she worked alongside a couple of others. Funny, she still pursued the task at hand with that same determined spirit he'd grown to love back in Bible college. How many times had he watched her dive into a project with such zeal? Nothing much had changed there, had it?

And yet, he had to admit as his gaze followed her, this was a much more mature woman standing before him. She handled herself with such professionalism. And even now, as he examined her handiwork, Chris couldn't help but think of how she might have fared on the mission field. Would she have worked alongside him with the people he'd grown to love in the outlying areas of Nicaragua? Would she have been willing to give all of this up to see his dream come true?

Snap out of it, Chris. He drew in a deep breath and called her name.

Adrianne turned abruptly, her face awash with surprise when she saw him. "Chris."

"Hey."

She nodded but said nothing, though her eyes registered

30

an interesting mix of excitement and nervousness. Was she happy to see him?

"I waited till lunch time to come," he said with a shrug. "I was hoping maybe. . ."

"Ah." She bit her lip, a habit he'd grown to love years ago.

"I was thinking maybe we could sneak off to the restaurant," he suggested. "Is that a possibility?"

She looked around, a look of anticipation on her face. "I guess that would work. But I can't be gone very long. We're trying to get this display finished before next week's fundraising dinner."

"Any amount of time you can give me will be great." His heart raced as the words were spoken. *Even two minutes with you would make my day.*

She stepped out of the display and ran her fingers through her somewhat messy hair. "I'm sure I look awful."

"No." He shook his head, unable to speak another word for fear the words would reveal too much of his heart. Instead, he reached up with a fingertip to help her brush a curl from her eyes.

Big mistake, Chris.

The minute his hand touched her hair, those old, familiar feelings returned. He let his palm rest against her brow for a second, his breaths coming a bit more slowly. Until this very moment, he hadn't realized just how much he missed her.

Adrianne's cheeks grew pink and she pulled away. Almost too abruptly, she turned and began to walk down the hallway in the direction of the bistro.

"So," she began. "You're in town for your friend's wedding."

"Yes. Stephen Madison."

"Ah. Friend from work?" She gave him an inquisitive look.

"Not really. I met him through the mission organization when I was raising funds to travel to Central America. He's done some amazing work with the Nicaraguan people, and that's partly because he grew up there. We've been close ever since the day we met, like brothers, really."

"Nicaragua." She whispered the word, and her face appeared to pale. He couldn't help but wonder why.

"Yes."

They arrived at the bistro and walked to the counter, where Chris turned to Adrianne. "What would you like to eat?"

She shook her head. "I'm not really hungry."

"Are you sure? Please eat with me." He put on his best puppy-dog face and she laughed, then ordered a turkey sandwich with Swiss on wheat.

"Mayo, not mustard." They spoke the words aloud, in unison, and she turned, her face reflecting genuine surprise.

"You remembered."

"There are a lot of things I remember." *Like how beautiful you look in blue. How those brown eyes sparkle when you get mad. How you love working like a maniac to get the job done. How you get silly if you stay up too late.* Chris wanted to say more, but when Adrianne's cheeks flashed pink, he turned, instead, to place his order.

When the food arrived, they made their way through the ever-growing lunch crowd to find a table. He spotted one off in the distance and gestured. Adrianne nodded and they eased through a group of kids to reach it.

"I've never seen so many elementary students in my life." He looked around the room in awe, the voices of children ringing out on every side.

"You should try coming on a Monday." Adrianne glanced down at the children and smiled. "It's pure chaos in here. Heavenly chaos."

As they sat next to each other at the small table, Chris turned to look at her one more time. Her eyes certainly lit with joy as she watched the children playing together. Not much had changed there, either. She'd always loved teaching the little ones at church, back in Virginia Beach. *She would be great on the mission field.* In his mind's eye, he could see her working with local children in the villages. They would take to her like flies to a piece of watermelon.

Just as quickly, he stopped himself, lest his hopes soar through the roof.

"I've thought about your work in Nicaragua a thousand times," she acknowledged, as if reading his mind.

His heart skipped a beat. "You have?"

Adrianne nodded. "In your last letter, you told me you were headed down there to work. I. . ." Her hands trembled as she opened her napkin. "I called the missions organization, hoping to find you, but you had already left."

"No way." He stared at her in disbelief. "You tried to track me down after I left? They never told me."

She shrugged. "I never gave them my name. And by the time I called, you were already there, out in the field, no less. I hated to bother you."

"Hated to bother me? Are you kidding? I would have flipped the world upside-down to get to a phone if I'd known you were trying to reach me. Didn't you know that?"

She stared down at the table. "Maybe. Maybe that was the part that scared me the most. I was so confused back then. Dealing with so much. . ."

As her voice trailed off, Chris couldn't help but notice a tear on the edge of her lashes. He reached to lift her chin and gazed into those haunting brown eyes. "You'll never know how much it means to me just to hear that you tried to reach me. Thank you for telling me." His fingertips traced the edge of her chin, and she leaned her cheek into his palm. Chris's heart quickened at her tender response.

"I. . ." He offered up a shrug. "I can't believe you never married."

He shook his head. "No. I couldn't."

"Couldn't?" She gave him an inquisitive look.

Chris pinched the napkin with his fingertips. "I. . ." He dared himself to speak the words. "I've never loved anyone but you. Not ever. I probably never will." Where the courage came from, he had no idea.

In response, her eyes seemed filled with love, and Chris knew, in that moment, she'd connected with his words.

"I'm so sorry," she whispered.

He reached to grasp her hands. "Sorry for what? We were two mixed-up kids who lost our focus. That's all."

"That's not all." A pained look filled her eyes, and she pulled away.

"What are you saying?"

"I–I'm. . ."

"Does this have something to do with what you were saying yesterday?" he asked. "You said you had something to tell me. Are you. . ." *Is she involved with someone else? Is she afraid to tell me?*

The hurt in her eyes let him know he'd crossed a line. At that point, a man he recognized as yesterday's tour guide appeared at the table. For whatever reason, Chris released Adrianne's hands immediately.

"Adrianne!"

Chris looked on in curiosity as Adrianne glanced up at her coworker.

"Hi, Joey." Her face lit into a smile.

A nervous energy laced Joey's words. "Is this private, or could I join you?"

If he sits down, I might have to punch his lights out.

"I, um. . ." Adrianne shrugged. "I think it might be better if you didn't right now. Chris and I are talking."

Thank You, Lord.

"Ah." Joey's eyes reflected his disappointment, but he moved on to another table.

"Sorry about that," Adrianne whispered. "W—where were we again?"

Chris shook his head, trying to figure out how to jump back into such a delicate conversation. He opted for a diversion, choosing instead to talk about the children he'd met on his various jaunts into the backwoods of Nicaragua. He told story after story, doing his best not to carry the full weight of the conversation.

Every now and again, Adrianne would chime in, giving her opinion or offering up an *ooh* or *ah*.

Finally, the moment arrived. Chris could delay no longer. His breath caught in his throat as the words raced out. "Stephen's wedding is Saturday afternoon, but there's a rehearsal dinner tomorrow night. It's late, after the rehearsal."

"Uh-huh." Her eyes reflected her curiosity.

"I was wondering. . ." *I want you to go with me. I want to spend every available minute with you, don't you see that?* "Would you go with me?"

Her lips pulled into a smile. "I'd love to."

Relief flooded his soul. "Thank you." He reached to give her hand a squeeze, though he couldn't help but notice the strained look from Joey, who sat a couple of tables away.

"I'll pick you up after the rehearsal," he started.

"No." Her abrupt answer threw him. "I, uh, it's not necessary for you to come to get me, not on such an important night. I can meet you."

"Are you sure?"

She gave a slight nod. "Yes. It's not a problem. I know this city like the back of my hand. It's the least I can do."

"Okay. Well, we've got reservations at the Penn's View Hotel. Do you know where that is?"

She nodded. "Of course. This is my city, remember?"

He nodded and smiled.

"I love that place," she said with a dreamy look on her face. "It's beautiful. Historic."

"Right. Well, just ask for the Conner party. That's the bride's last name. We'll be in the restaurant—the Ristorante Panorama." He loved saying the words; their Latin flavor reminded him at once of the language that flowed like water from his lips as he labored alongside his Nicaraguan coworkers.

Though he'd only been back in the States a couple of weeks, he already missed the excitement of the language. And he missed the people, though he hadn't acknowledged that to anyone aloud. If only Adrianne would marry him—go back there with him—they would work together to reach the people and—

"Mmm. They have great veal." Adrianne's eyes sparkled mischievously.

Chris shook himself out of his dream state. He could hardly think about food. Not right now. Not when she'd just agreed to spend the evening with him. He tried to calm his heart as he continued on. "Come around eight o'clock, okay?"

"I'll be there." Adrianne glanced at her watch and pushed back her chair with an anxious look. "I have to get back to work."

"I understand." *But not yet. Please. One more thing.* Chris reached to grab Adrianne's hand one last time and the words just flowed. "Adrianne, I need to know that you've forgiven me. Please. I have to know."

"I told you yesterday."

"I know, but. . ." He drew in a deep breath. "I need to hear the words. I have to hear them before I can move on."

For a moment, neither of them said anything. Eventually moisture rimmed the edges of Adrianne's lashes and she dabbed at her eyes with her napkin. "God has forgiven me of so much." Her hoarse whisper seemed to grate across her throat. "How could I not forgive you?"

Chris worked to push back the lump in his throat as he thanked her.

She looked at him dead-on. "It's not that easy, Chris. I need your forgiveness, too."

He shook his head. "No. No, you don't."

"I do," she whispered. "You'll never know how much."

He gave her hand a loving squeeze. "Adrianne, you've got it. I forgive you. Though, for the life of me, I don't know what I'm forgiving you for."

❮❯

"I don't know what I'm forgiving you for."

Adrianne pondered Chris's words for hours after they parted ways. For some reason, she couldn't shake the image of his eyes—eyes that reminded her in every way of Lorelei's—from her mind.

Soon, he would know the truth. She would tell him. Tomorrow night.

six

"Mom, you look so pretty!" Lorelei joined Adrianne at the mirror and stared in exaggerated admiration.

"Do you like my dress?" Adrianne twirled in a circle for effect.

"Mm-hmm." The youngster gave a brisk nod. "Is it new?"

"Sort of. I bought it for the fundraiser dinner next week, but decided it was too pretty to wear only once."

"So, where are you going?" Lorelei asked, her innocent eyes staring up in awe. "Someplace special?"

To see your daddy.

For the first time, the word *daddy* sent a shockwave through Adrianne. Soon—tonight, in fact—Chris would know he was a daddy. And soon enough, Lorelei would meet her father. *Lord, help me. I've already made such a mess of things. I only want to make things better now. . . .*

"I–I'm going to a restaurant in a fancy hotel to meet an old friend," Adrianne said with a forced smile.

"A *man* friend?" Lorelei asked, her eyes dancing with excitement.

Adrianne sighed. "Yes. A man friend."

"Mom!" Lorelei's face lit up even more, if that were possible. "Is it a date? A real, honest-to-goodness date?"

"Good grief, you're full of questions." *If I tell her it's a date, she'll have me married off by night's end.* "It's just dinner with an old friend. Don't fill your head with all sorts of ideas, promise?"

"I promise." The youngster's smile shifted to a frown. "But

38

Grandma says you need to start dating. She says—"

"Never mind all that now." Adrianne tried to put a stop to the conversation. "You'd better get busy with your homework. We'll be leaving soon."

"Am I going with you?" Lorelei's eyes broadened to saucer-width.

"Um, no." *Not hardly.* "You're staying with your grand-parents. But homework comes first. So get busy now, while I finish dressing."

Her daughter reluctantly left the room, and Adrianne completed the task of putting on her jewelry and makeup. She shot one last glance in the mirror before leaving. *I've aged so much since our college days, Chris. How in the world you might still find me attractive remains a mystery.*

Immediately, Lorelei appeared at her side. "Mom, you're the prettiest lady I know."

Her words startled Adrianne. *Were you listening in on my thoughts again, you little imp?* She reached down to give her daughter a hug. "I'm not sure I'd agree, but I appreciate you for saying that. Kind of makes an old woman feel young again to be told she's pretty."

"You're not old." Lorelei giggled.

Adrianne sighed as she glanced in the mirror, wondering if Chris thought she looked older. *Stop worrying about that,* she chided herself. *Stay focused.*

At that very moment her cell phone rang. Adrianne's heart flip-flopped as she contemplated the possibilities. *Is it Chris?*

She answered it on the third ring, but her heart sank as she heard James Kenner's voice instead.

"Hi, Adrianne, I hope I'm not interrupting anything."

"Oh, I. . .well, I'm just getting ready to go out."

"Ah." His downcast voice caught her off guard. "I guess it's too late to ask you to dinner then."

Ask me to dinner? "Well, I have plans to meet an old friend," she explained.

"No problem. I was just thinking it would be fun to get together and talk about the plans for the fundraiser dinner. I know Bob Martinson wanted my input."

"Oh?" Why in the world would her boss want James Kenner's input regarding the dinner?

"Well, I can see you're busy," James said. "I won't keep you. Maybe one of these days we can get together. Soon, I hope."

"M—maybe." She thanked him for the invitation and quickly ended the call.

"Was that him, Mom?" Lorelei asked.

"No."

"Who was it?"

"Someone else. Someone from work."

"Oh." Lorelei's downcast face spoke volumes.

Adrianne finished the task of getting ready. Soon thereafter, she and Lorelei headed out for the evening. "Did you get that homework done?" she asked as they climbed into the car.

"Almost."

"I hope you brought it with you then. Make sure you finish it."

"Grandpa will help me. He likes spelling."

"Yes, he does."

Adrianne tried to stay focused on her daughter's words, but found her mind drifting to the inevitable. She looked over at Lorelei and drew in a deep breath. *Lord, help me through this night.*

Forty-five minutes later, Adrianne stood outside the beautiful, historic Penn's View Hotel. A bellman met her at the door.

"Good evening, miss."

" 'Evening." She offered a polite nod. "I'm meeting friends at the Panorama. A wedding party."

"Just down the hall to your left." He gestured, and then

shifted his attention to another customer.

Adrianne took in the beauty of the place as she made her way down the elegant hallway. She loved Philadelphia so much, particularly the exquisite historic buildings like this one. It wasn't just the architecture, though that certainly took her breath away. It was the fact that so many amazing things had happened here throughout the years. History was made in places like this.

Perhaps tonight's meeting would make the history books, too. At least the ones featuring her life story.

Within a minute or two, she stood at the entrance of the lovely restaurant. A hostess, dressed in black, met her with a smile. "Can I help you?"

"Yes. I'm here to meet the Conner party."

"Ah. The wedding party."

Wedding party. Why did the words shake her? "Yes."

"They called from the church to say they'd run into a bit of a problem. Something about the minister not showing up for the rehearsal on time. They'll be here shortly. Would you like me to seat you?"

"Um, no thank you." She looked around, feeling a little lost. "I think I'll just look around the hotel a few minutes."

Disappointed, Adrianne turned back toward the hall with a sigh on her lips.

❧

"Can't you drive any faster?"

"What's your hurry, Chris?" Stephen asked. "You'd think this was your rehearsal dinner, not mine."

"Sorry." Chris glanced down at his watch: 8:23. Would Adrianne still be at the restaurant, or would she have given up already and headed home? He prayed it was not the latter.

"It's that girl, isn't it?" Stephen looked over with a crooked grin. "Adrianne?"

"Yeah."

"Don't worry. She'll still be there. How could she leave my good buddy hanging in the lurch?"

It wouldn't be the first time. Chris thought back to the day she'd left Virginia Beach. "I just don't want to take any chances. I really feel like God has given me an opportunity here, and I don't want to blow it."

"Then listen up." Stephen's voice grew serious. "If it's really God, you won't have to worry about what you do or don't do. This is in His hands. His. Meaning, you couldn't blow it if you wanted to."

"I'm not so sure about that."

"I'd like to go on record as saying"—Stephen looked over at him with a mischievous grin—"the next wedding will be your own."

I pray you're right.

"Then we'll be sitting in traffic with your bride-to-be three cars back with a group of chattering, overdressed bridesmaids, and you and I will be driving together with the guys. Again."

"Yeah. I hope so, anyway."

Stephen dove into a complicated speech about marriage, and Chris tried to relax. His friend was right, at least about the part where Adrianne would still be at the restaurant, waiting. If the Lord was in this thing. And if He wasn't. . .

If He wasn't, Chris thought perhaps his heart would break in two.

seven

Adrianne's nerves reached the breaking point as Chris and the others rounded the corner. *Lord, help me through this night. Please.* The look in Chris's eyes made things all the more intriguing, which certainly didn't serve to calm her down in the slightest.

He took her by the hand and shook his head, almost as if he couldn't believe his eyes. "You're. . .breathtaking."

She felt her cheeks warm, and she tried to shush him, but he would not be silenced.

"No, you're absolutely beautiful." His eyes brimmed over, and she was glad for the distraction of the maitre d' seating them.

Chris made introductions as they took their seats. Stephen and his bride-to-be, Julie, welcomed Adrianne, and she offered profuse thanks for the invitation.

"We're happy to have you." Julie gave her a knowing smile. "I really believe it's a God-thing, don't you? I mean, how romantic that the two of you would meet again after all these years."

Adrianne felt her cheeks flush as she offered up a mumbled response. Did everyone here see her as a potential love interest for Chris?

Did *she*?

Within minutes, everyone in the wedding party chattered merrily, but Adrianne and Chris only had eyes for each other. They reminisced, talking about college professors, courses they'd taken, and their common dislike for math.

At one point, Stephen chided his best man with a "Hey, glad you could join us, Chris," but even that did little to pull the two apart. Adrianne didn't mind the noise going on around them. In fact, other than the beat of her pulse in her ears and the lulling sound of Chris's voice as he shared his stories, she heard nothing. Absolutely nothing.

And still, as the evening wore on, one problem remained. The obvious. The inevitable.

Just as the dessert arrived, Adrianne took Chris by the hand. He gave it a squeeze and stared into her eyes.

Her gaze shifted at once to the table. "I have something to tell you." The words vibrated in sync with her hands.

"Tell me." He gave her fingertips a loving squeeze. "Whatever it is, you can tell me."

She shook her head. "I need to know if you'll come to my parents' house with me for a little while. We can talk there."

He gave her a curious look. "O—okay."

"I'll bring you back to the hotel after." Adrianne tried to keep her breaths steady, but her heart continued to race. "I promise. But I need you to come with me. And I know my mom and dad have been looking forward to seeing you."

"You told them I was here?"

"Yeah."

"It will be good to see your parents again," he acknowledged. "I've missed them a lot."

"They've missed you, too." Adrianne started to push back her chair, but Chris leaped to his feet to assist her.

"You're ready to go? Right now?"

"Mm-hmm." As she stood to her feet, the cloth napkin floated to the ground. Her heart seemed to hit the floor alongside it.

He reached down to pick it up, a gesture of kindness. "I, um. . ." He glanced over at the others. "I just need to tell

Stephen. I know he's expecting me to stay here at the hotel with the rest of the guys."

"I'm sorry. Do you mind?"

"No. It's not a problem." Chris leaned over to whisper something into Stephen's ear.

Adrianne watched as the two men exchanged a quiet conversation, then Chris gave Stephen a quick shrug as he looked her way. *Sorry.* She mouthed the word. She hated to interrupt the fellow's rehearsal dinner, but she simply couldn't put this off one moment longer. Her heart wouldn't allow it. She'd waited eight years too long. Not one second more would do.

Julie looked her way. "Leaving so soon?"

"If you don't mind." Adrianne reached to give her a hug. "Thanks so much for having me."

"Thank you for coming. Will we see you tomorrow?"

"Oh, I, uh. . ."

"Please say you'll be there, and come to the reception, too. You can bring a friend if you like, if it would make you more comfortable."

Adrianne shrugged. "I don't know."

Someone called out the bride's name and her attention shifted. Adrianne and Chris took advantage of the opportunity to slip out of the room. Moments later, they pulled away from the hotel in her car. She shivered against the chill.

"Cold?" Chris reached to turn on the heater.

She shook her head. *Not cold. Just a sudden, horrifying case of nerves.*

Her foot vibrated against the accelerator as she pulled out onto the turnpike.

"So, we're going to your parents' house," Chris started. "Do you live with them?"

"No. I have my own place."

"Ah."

"There's something I need to take care of there." She whispered the words. "Something big."

Chris sat in silence, but she felt his gaze as it bore a hole into her heart. *He's got to be wondering what in the world is wrong with me.*

A painful silence filled the car for a couple of minutes. Chris broke it with a question. "I've always wondered if you went back to school."

She startled to attention. "W—what?"

"I mean, you left just after starting your senior year. I've always wondered if you finished up, got your degree."

"Oh. Yes, actually, I did." She didn't give him any details. Perhaps later she would tell him about going back to school in Philly the year after Lorelei was born. One thing at a time.

Adrianne tried to shift the conversation back to Stephen's wedding, but she didn't do a very good job. Her words surely sounded strained. Contrived. Chris must've picked up on her subdued mood, because his light-hearted responses all but disappeared.

Within minutes, she pulled up in front of her mom and dad's house, parking just underneath the street light. Chris unlatched his seatbelt and started to open his door, but she reached across to take his hand in an attempt to stop him. "Wait. Please wait."

He turned to face her. "You're scaring me, Adrianne."

She tried to force back the lump in her throat but it would not be squelched. It, along with the tears that now rose to her lashes, gave her away. "Chris, I need to tell you something. It's something I should have told you years ago. Something I *tried* to tell you years ago."

He offered up a silent stare, along with a shrug. The blank look in his eyes spoke of his desire to understand. She would make him understand.

Adrianne closed her eyes and whispered a prayer. *Oh Lord, please help me through this. I want Your will. I'm so sorry for taking things into my own hands.*

"When I left that note under your door," she started, "it was because I knew I had to leave Virginia Beach."

Chris nodded. "I know. You told me."

"No." She shook her head. "You don't know. You know only half the story. I had to leave because. . ."

The tears came full force now, and Chris leaned over to slip his arm around her shoulder. She wondered if she should shrug it away, or give in to the comfort it brought.

"Were you in love with someone else?" he whispered, his voice strained.

"No." She gazed up into his eyes. They were filled with pain. *Oh Father. They're about to be filled with even more pain, aren't they?* "I never loved anyone but you. I never have."

Relief flooded his face and he drew her close. "Then tell me, Adrianne. Whatever it is, I can deal with it. Were you sick? Had something happened back home?"

She shook her head and drew in a deep breath. "No." The words flowed now. She couldn't have stopped them if she'd tried. "I—I left Virginia Beach because I was pregnant."

He stared in stunned silence. "W–what?" His arm loosened around her shoulder and he pulled back, a look of horror in his eyes.

"I was pregnant," she whispered. "With your baby." This time, she didn't give him time to ask questions. She raced through the story, feeling it afresh as the words tumbled forth like those autumn leaves of that awful day so long ago. "I left Virginia Beach the day I found out. I couldn't think straight. I came home to be with my parents. I knew they would help me, tell me what to do."

"But, Adrianne. . ." She read the rejection in his eyes as he pulled away. "You. . .you. . ." He shook his head, unable to continue as tears filled his eyes.

"I'm so sorry." The words sounded lame, even to her.

"You had no right to do that—just leave without telling me? You. . ." His voice trailed off. "You should have come to me. I would have done the right thing."

"I know that." She hung her head in shame. "But I was so young, and so scared. You have no idea how scared. I knew you were headed to the mission field. And the mission board wouldn't have let you go. Not if they'd known the truth. It would have ruined everything for you."

"That's. . ." He shook his head, and anger laced his words. "That's ridiculous. W—we could have *made* it work."

She shook her head. "No. You would have given up on your dream."

"*You* were my dream." He spoke the words so emphatically, they scared her. "You. Yes, I wanted to work on the mission field, but my ultimate goal was for the two of us to minister together, to work hand in hand. When I left for Nicaragua, I felt emptier than I'd ever felt. Part of it was the fact that I'd drifted from God, at least in part. I thought being there would fill the emptiness, but it didn't."

"I—I'm sorry." She whispered the words.

"And your explanation makes it sound like you did all of this *for* me. That's. . .ludicrous." His pensive stare sent daggers through her heart. She wanted to respond, but no words would come.

For a moment, neither of them said a word. Finally, he asked the dreaded question. "Th—the baby?"

Adrianne's heart lifted a bit as she shifted her conversation to Lorelei. "She was born that next spring."

"She?"

"Yes. Lorelei. She was born in April."

"Lorelei." He whispered the word. "Like the Lorelei that we learned about in Lit class? The one who sang along the rocks of the Rhine River?"

Adrianne nodded. "I knew you loved that story."

Chris's voice seemed to tighten even further, if that were possible. "So my daughter was born in April. I was still in school in April. You could have called me. You *should* have called me. I would have come to Philadelphia. I would have flown halfway around the world to be with her." He choked back tears. "With you."

"I know, I know." Adrianne leaned her face into her palms and wept openly. How many times had she picked up the phone to call? Ten? Twenty?

"You said you got my letters," he whispered. "And you still didn't tell me? Why? You knew I loved you. You knew it. And you. . .you *stole* this from me?"

"I'm so sorry." She took a breath. "I was so, so scared. I knew I would eventually tell you. And I tried to. I really did."

"You tried to? When? How? I'm just not seeing it, Adrianne."

"That June, when Lorelei was still tiny, I tried to call your apartment. It was something my dad said that gave me the courage. He told me that from the day I was born, his heart would swell with pride whenever he looked at me. He said he would always think to himself, 'There's my little daddy's girl.' So I called. I did. June 24. Lorelei was two months old that day."

"June 24." He whispered the words. "I'd already left for Nicaragua."

"Yes." *Oh Lord, please help him understand.* "I talked to your roommate. He told me you'd left. I never told him why I was calling, but he was great. He gave me the number for the mission organization in Managua. I called them that same day. Remember, I told you. . . ."

"Yes, you told me you called them, but you left out a very

important detail. You never told me *why* you called." His breaths were coming quicker now. She could hear them and could sense the strain in his voice.

"I–I'm sorry, Chris. I am. But. . ."

He shook his head and anger laced his words. "They could have reached me. Might have taken some doing, but they could have reached me."

"Yes," she said, "but I couldn't relay a message like that through other people. This was something I had to do myself."

Chris leaned back against the seat and closed his eyes. Adrianne reached over to grasp his hand.

"Chris. . ." She gave him an imploring look. "Don't you see? You were already there, doing what you were called to do. I was here, and things were going okay. My parents were helping me. It would have been wrong to stop you midstream. I should have told you sooner, not later."

"So, you decided not to tell me at all?" His words carried an icy chill. "You were going to let me go the rest of my life not knowing I had a daughter? You felt that was the answer?"

Adrianne shook her head, trying to explain. "No. When your letters kept coming, I tried again. I called your parents' home."

"You did?" His voice had an air of disbelief, but Adrianne couldn't blame him. "When?"

"Your father had just passed away. Your mother was very broken. Hurting. She said that you would only be back in the States long enough to attend the funeral. The timing was. . . awful."

Chris nodded.

"I tried again when Lorelei was three." Adrianne smiled, remembering. "My parents had been praying all the while that you and I would. . .well. . ."

He gave her a curious stare.

"They really loved you."

"In spite of my flaws?"

"They always loved you. Still do."

"Even though I got their daughter pregnant?"

Adrianne sighed. "They're grace-filled people. More so than I deserve." She sat a moment, remembering the love her parents had poured out on her those first few years. "I tried to track you down in Nicaragua, the year Lorelei turned three," she continued. "By then we were told you'd moved on to a different organization. No one in Managua had your contact information. It was like a trail of evidence leading. . .nowhere. But I wanted to find you. I always wanted to find you."

The sound of Adrianne's heart pounding in her ears proved deafening. "If I *had* found you," she said finally, "I'm not sure what I would have said. How I would have said it. It would have been so. . .so hard."

"What are we going to do?" He gave her a blank stare. Underneath the lamplight, his eyes seemed vacant, hollow.

Adrianne gave a little shiver. "I think we need to take this one step at a time. First things first. You need to meet your daughter."

He shook his head without responding.

Please don't say you won't see her.

"Does she know about me?" he asked quietly. "Does she even know I exist?"

"Yes, she knows she has a daddy." Adrianne chose her words carefully. She'd been very limited in what she'd told Lorelei, naturally.

"But does she know I'm here? In Philadelphia?"

Adrianne shook her head. "I couldn't think of a way to tell her. I needed to tell you first. But my parents know. They've been praying for this day for years."

More silence.

Then, with a deep sigh, Chris turned his gaze toward the house. "They're probably wondering what we're doing out here."

"No. I'm sure they've figured it out. They'll want to spend a few minutes with us before we wake Lorelei."

"Lorelei." He whispered the word again, then leaned back against the seat and closed his eyes. "Lorelei."

The sound of their daughter's name running across his lips was pure music to Adrianne's ears.

eight

The trembling in Chris's hands hadn't stopped for a good ten minutes, ever since receiving the news.

I am a father.

I have a daughter.

The words hadn't fully permeated his heart, at least at this point. He wondered if they ever would. In fact, as he eased his way out of the front seat of Adrianne's car, he contemplated pinching himself. Would he wake up from this dream-like state to discover life was exactly as it had been ten minutes before?

No.

One pinch was all it took.

As they made their way up the front walk to the door of Adrianne's parents' home, Chris fought to understand. Why would she have kept this from him? *How* she could have kept this from him? How she could have kept his *child* from him?

Just as quickly, guilt swept in. His sin, the very thing he'd agonized over for the past eight years, had caught up with him. There was no simple apology. No asking for forgiveness and watching it go away.

No, in this case there were certainly consequences.

If you could call a child a consequence.

All of these things, and more, filled his head as they approached the front door. The silence nearly deafened him. He wanted to yell. At the top of his lungs. Wanted to cry out to God. . .to Adrianne. . .to anyone who would listen.

Instead, his lips remained sealed.

But his heart did not. In fact, it felt as if it had been ripped from top to bottom. Chris wasn't sure if he'd ever felt such raw pain before. Or betrayal.

Yes, Adrianne. Betrayal. You lied to me. You stole seven years of my daughter's life from me.

Just as quickly, his anger shifted to joy. When he contemplated the truth—that he had a daughter just beyond that door—his heart nearly burst with anticipation.

"A–are you ready?" Adrianne whispered, as if in response to his thoughts. She lifted her key to place it in the door.

"Wait." Chris reached to touch her arm, needing just a minute more. "I have to know this. Is she. . .is she like me? In any way at all?"

Under the porch light, he could see Adrianne's face come alive. "Oh, Chris. . ." A glistening of tears tipped over the edges of her lashes as she spoke. "Your daughter is the spitting image of you. She has your features, your hair. . ." Adrianne's lips turned up in a loving smile. "Your goofy personality. Especially that. She's funny, Chris. A real clown sometimes. But smart. Really smart. And she has the most giving heart you've ever seen. Just like you."

He pressed down the lump in his throat as he nodded his head. "Does she know the Lord? Have you. . .?"

Strangely, in light of his past sin, the question seemed oddly out of place. And yet he had to know.

"She knows." Adrianne grinned. "She's very passionate about her faith, especially for being so young. I told you, she's so much like you it hurts."

Hurts. A word I understand.

"Are you ready?"

He offered up a lame nod, and Adrianne opened the door to the living room. Almost immediately, her mother and father swept him into their arms. He heard his name from both their lips, but their excitement made it nearly impossible to distinguish one voice from the other.

Finally, Mrs. Russo paused long enough to plant a kiss on his cheek. "We thought this day would never come." She put her hand over her mouth and shook her head in silence.

"Son. . ." Mr. Russo extended a hand. "We're glad to see you."

Why? How in the world could you not hate me?

As if in response, Adrianne's father wrestled him into a tight bear hug. He could feel the man's chest begin to heave, and sobs came. For both of them. Soon enough, they were all four in tears. Mrs. Russo ushered them to the sofa, where they sat in a puddle until someone finally broke through the ruckus.

"What happened? Grandma? Mama?"

Chris looked up through tear-stained eyes at the beautiful little girl who'd just entered the room. Her light brown hair glistened under the lamplight and as she rubbed at her eyes with the backs of her hands, he couldn't help but notice the color of those eyes. Green. Same as his. Immediately, his hand went to his mouth, and he fought to keep from crying aloud.

"Lorelei." Adrianne rose from the couch and stepped in the child's direction. "We didn't mean to wake you, baby."

"I heard crying." The youngster looked around the room, a sleepy expression on her face. "What happened?"

"Oh. . ." Mrs. Russo stood and ran her fingers through Lorelei's hair and forced a smile. "We're just happy. You know, adults cry sometimes when they're happy."

Lorelei didn't look convinced. "What are you all so happy about?" Her gaze shifted from person to person until it came to land on Chris. His heart flew into his throat the minute their eyes locked. For a moment, no one said anything. Finally, Adrianne spoke up.

"Lorelei, this is the friend I told you about. Chris."

"Ooh." Lorelei's eyes widened in merriment. "The one you went on the date with?"

Chris couldn't hide his smile.

"Um, well, yes." Adrianne nodded. "We went to dinner together."

"He looks like that man in the picture, Mom." Lorelei took a step in his direction, but Chris's gaze shifted at once to Adrianne.

"What picture?" Adrianne's eyes grew large.

"You know." Lorelei crossed her arms, a pensive look on her face. "That picture you hide in your underwear drawer."

Chris's heart almost sang aloud at her words. So, she had been thinking about him. Even after all these years, she'd kept his picture close by.

Adrianne leaned her head into her hands, then looked up with a sheepish smile. "Yeah, he does kind of look like that guy, doesn't he?"

"Mm-hmm." She—his daughter, his Lorelei—gave him another once-over and he attempted a smile.

Mrs. Russo opted to shift gears, though her red-rimmed eyes still gave her away. "I've got a German chocolate cake in the kitchen. Anyone hungry?"

Chris didn't know that he could ever eat another bite of food as long as he lived, but he followed along on her heels as she led them into the kitchen. All the while, he stared at the remarkable youngster to his right. *My daughter. My little girl.* His heart swelled until he thought it would burst. Suddenly, much of the anger he'd felt—even the sting of betrayal— seemed to lessen. When he looked at this little angel, he was suddenly filled with possibilities, nothing else.

As they settled down at the table, Lorelei chattered merrily about a dream she'd been having before they'd awakened her. Something about singing on a big stage somewhere. He couldn't seem to focus on her story. No, he was blown away by her very presence. She looked remarkably like Adrianne.

And yet she shared so many of his characteristics, right down to the eye color and the hair. The nose was Adrianne's, to be sure. And the lyrical sound of her laughter. Just like her mother.

At one point, she looked his way, cheeks flaming pink as she announced, "My mom wore her brand-new dress just for you."

"She did?" Chris peered over at Adrianne, whose expression still seemed guarded.

Adrianne nodded. "Yeah. I did."

"*I* want to get dressed up and go out on a date," Lorelei said with a pout.

"Oh no. You're never dating." Chris and Mr. Russo spoke in unison. Chris clamped a hand to his mouth the moment the words were spoken. Where had they come from?

Lorelei gave him a quizzical look. "How come?"

"Well, I, um. . ." He looked to Adrianne for support.

"When you're old enough," she explained, "then you can date."

"But I want to look pretty like my mom." Lorelei leaped from her seat and pressed herself into her mother's lap, where at once she began to play with Adrianne's hair.

Adrianne's mom chuckled. "You don't have to date to look pretty. You look pretty right now."

You're beautiful, in fact.

"I want my mom's hair."

Chris watched it all in silence, his throat suddenly constricted. *My daughter and my. . .* The word *wife* entered his mind but then disappeared just as quickly. *Lord, you know my heart. You know my greatest desire right now is for—*

"No one has prettier hair than you." Adrianne buried her face into Lorelei's hair after speaking the words. Her tears started again. She wept in silence, but Lorelei wasn't fooled.

"Are you happy again, Mom?"

Adrianne glanced across the table at Chris and nodded. "I am."

"She must really like you a lot." Lorelei bounced from her mom's lap and approached him. Chris wanted to scoop her up into his arms, wanted to plant kisses on her forehead. Wanted to tell her that he loved her—more than life itself.

Instead, he nodded lamely. "I like her a lot, too."

"You do?" Lorelei's eyes grew large as she turned to face her mother. "He likes you a lot."

Adrianne brushed away the tears and nodded without responding.

Say something, Adrianne. Say that you love me. . .that we're supposed to be together. Say that. . .

"It's way past your bedtime." As Adrianne stood, the bottom of the chair legs scraped against the tile floor with a squeal. "We should be getting home."

"Do we have to go?" Lorelei whimpered.

Chris's heart echoed her sentiments. He didn't want to go. He didn't ever want to leave this room for fear he would lose everything he had suddenly gained.

And yet another world awaited. The wedding. Tomorrow afternoon. Downtown. He had to be there for Stephen, had to fulfill his obligation.

Fulfill your obligation.

For the first time, he thought about the fact that Adrianne and her family had taken on both the emotional and financial obligation of raising Lorelei up to this point. He would change that. Immediately. He would make sure she was taken care of, that she had everything she needed and more.

Whoa. Slow down, man. You can't change everything in one night.

Lorelei flashed her mother a woeful smile, in an attempt to

sway her, no doubt. "Can't we just stay here tonight? Puh-leeze?"

"I have to get Chris back to the hotel."

"Oh! We're driving you?" Lorelei turned to look his way.

"Looks like it," he said, not even trying to hide the smile.

"You sit up front with my mom," the youngster instructed. "I'll sit in the back."

You little matchmaker, you.

"That's up to your mama."

Chris looked at Adrianne, and for the first time saw her through new eyes. She was more than a creative soul, a hard worker, a museum curator. She was. . .a mother. The mother of his child. And she had done a remarkable job of raising this little girl, even without his help.

He swallowed back the pain at the thought of those last few words. He would make up for the lack of help now, if it was the last thing he did.

"Son, it was good to see you." Another bear hug from Adrianne's father felt awfully good, especially in light of the fact that Chris had lost his own father just a few years ago. He pondered that fact for a moment.

I've been without a father.

My daughter has been without a father.

A shiver ran through him as he embraced Adrianne's dad one more time. "I'm so glad to be here." He wanted to say more, but feared he would give away too much in front of Lorelei.

After a hug from Adrianne's mother, they were on their way. True to her word, Lorelei climbed into the back seat, allowing him the front, though he suddenly felt awkward next to Adrianne. Everything had changed over the past hour. Everything.

As Adrianne drove, Lorelei chattered merrily from behind. Chris didn't mind. In fact, the more she talked, the less he needed to, which served his purposes just fine, at least for now. When they arrived at the hotel, he turned to face Adrianne, wanting to say so many things, but unable to speak a word beyond the obvious "Good night."

She gave him an imploring look and reached for his hand. He took it, though mixed feelings still threatened to consume him.

As he climbed out of the car, Lorelei waved from the backseat.

"G'night, Chris! See you soon!" she said with a giggle.

"Yes. See you soon."

The car pulled away, and Chris's heart immediately plummeted. Somehow, in one night, he had gained—and lost—almost everything.

nine

Adrianne pulled away from the hotel, but a piece of her heart remained behind—with Chris. She couldn't bear the thought of leaving him like this, with no clear resolution. No plan. And yet, what choice did she have? They couldn't exactly talk things through in front of Lorelei.

Lorelei. She looked over at her daughter, praying she would fall asleep. Nope. No such luck. Instead, the youngster seemed to have come alive in Chris's presence.

She's drawn to him. But then she would be. Wouldn't she?

"I like Chris a lot, Mom." Her daughter gave a little giggle, then leaned back against the seat with a deep sigh. "Don't you?"

"Yes, honey, I do. He's a really nice man." Adrianne kept her eyes focused on the road, but her mind wandered all over the place.

"And he's handsome, too!" At this, Lorelei's spurts of laughter grew more animated. "Like the prince in Cinderella."

"Oh, and I suppose he has a glass slipper just my size." Adrianne chuckled at the thought of it.

"Maybe." Lorelei grew silent for a moment, then spoke quite seriously. "You're always losing your shoes, anyway. You *need* a prince."

Adrianne groaned. "Puh-leeze. You've been watching too many movies. It doesn't really happen like that. Not in the real world."

"Grandma says it does."

"Good grief." *How can I argue with that?*

Another sigh escaped Lorelei's lips. "And he likes you, Mom. I can tell."

"Oh?" Adrianne caught her breath, lest she say too much. "Now, how can you tell a thing like that?"

"He said so. Besides, he looks at you a lot," Lorelei explained. "And his eyes are smiling."

"Oh, his *eyes* are smiling, are they?"

"Mm-hmm. When will we see him again? Can he come over for dinner tomorrow night?"

"He's in a wedding tomorrow," Adrianne explained.

"He's getting married?" The disappointment in the youngster's voice was keen. "No way."

"His *friend* is getting married."

"Ooh. Okay." Lorelei's voice took on a dreamy quality. "Maybe he can come over the next night?"

Adrianne pulled the car into the entrance of their apartment complex and fumbled for her remote control to open the gate. "Maybe. We'll see."

"Promise you'll ask."

"I promise."

Adrianne couldn't help but smile at her daughter's persistence. Just as quickly, the somber reality resurfaced, taking the place of the joy. She and Chris needed to talk—and soon. Yes, his reaction had been better than expected. He hadn't blown up at the news, though she'd worried over it for eight years. His reaction had been. . .reasonable. That was the word. At least he hadn't turned and run in the opposite direction. Yet.

As they walked toward their apartment door, Lorelei let out an exaggerated yawn.

Adrianne reached over to pat her on the head. "Sleepy?"

"No."

Yes you are, you little goof. Just too stubborn to admit it.

"What are we going to do tomorrow?"

"Well. . ." Adrianne thought for a moment. "The leaves are changing. Why don't we go to the park and take some pictures? I'll use my new digital camera."

"Okay." Another yawn slipped out.

They entered the apartment, and Lorelei dressed for bed.

"Is there any particular reason you chose the Cinderella nightgown?"

Lorelei just giggled.

Adrianne couldn't help but laugh. "Fine. I get your message. But enough with playing around, okay?"

"Okay."

"Brush your teeth, and then we'll say our prayers."

The youngster headed off into the bathroom. Less than a minute later, however, she emerged with toothbrush in hand, her eyes twinkling. "What's Chris's last name, Mom?" she asked, a look of innocence in her eyes.

"Bradley."

"Adrianne Bradley." The youngster giggled. "I like it." Almost immediately, however, her expression changed. "But I'll still be Russo?"

Yikes. How in the world do I respond to that? Adrianne put on her most serious face. "You've got me married off already?" she asked, hoping to shift gears. "Don't you think it's a little early for that?"

Lorelei shrugged. "I dunno." She went back into the bathroom for a couple of minutes, then emerged again, this time with toothpaste smeared all over her lips. "Still, if you got married, he could adopt me. Right?"

"Could we talk about this tomorrow?" Adrianne didn't even try to stop the groan that escaped from the back of her throat. "I've got a terrible headache." In all honestly, her head did hurt. And if anyone deserved a few moments of peace and quiet, she did. Especially in light of all she'd been through this evening.

Lorelei gazed up with an imploring look. "Can I sleep with you tonight, Mom?"

Oh, not tonight. Tonight I need to be alone, to think, to pray. . .

"I promise not to steal the covers." Lorelei's sheepish giggle did little to sway her.

"I really do have a headache," Adrianne explained. "So I think it's best if you. . ."

The look of sadness that swept over her daughter's face did the trick.

"Oh, okay. But just tonight. I don't want you to get in the habit."

"Thank you, thank you!" Lorelei jumped up and down, and Adrianne immediately put her finger over her lips to shush the youngster, lest Mr. Sanderson take to pounding on the wall again.

"Promise you'll go to sleep right away?"

"I promise." She gave a little twirl and the Cinderella nightie caught Adrianne's eye one last time. Perhaps there would be a "happily ever after" in both their lives. If only. . .

Hmm. There were too many if-only possibilities to ponder right now. Instead, she tucked her daughter in for the night and they prayed together. Then, after just a few minutes, Lorelei's words grew slower, quieter. Finally, her breaths came in long, steady succession, and Adrianne knew she'd fallen asleep.

At this point, Adrianne quietly dressed for bed and slid under the covers alongside her daughter. As she leaned back against the pillows, the tears threatened to come again. She tried to push them back, but finally relinquished. It might do her good to cry, all things considered.

Still, she must do it silently. And with as little movement as possible. Not an easy task.

After a few moments, she dried her eyes and tried to rest.

Her mind would not be silenced. So many questions to be answered. . .

Will Chris forgive me?

Will he want to get to know his daughter?

She took her hand and gently ran it across Lorelei's back. The youngster stirred, then settled back down again.

How will I tell her? How will we tell her?

This was not the first time she'd worried about Lorelei's reaction to the news. Adrianne had played out multiple scenarios in her mind over the years. Still, she couldn't come to grips with how—or when—to tell her. Up until now, Lorelei had asked very little about her father, only once or twice questioning his existence. Adrianne had managed to get by with a limited explanation of his work in another country.

But now. . .

She's going to put it together. She's a smart little girl. And she's seen his photograph. It's only a matter of time before she. . .

Her prayer came in rushed whispers, more mouthed than spoken aloud: "Lord, I've made such a mess of everything. I've asked Chris to forgive me. I know one day Lorelei will have to learn to forgive me, too. But tonight, Father, I ask for Your forgiveness. Forgive me for not doing the right thing in the first place. Forgive me for keeping Lorelei from her father. I should have told him right away. Then she would have known him. I've taken that from her."

A familiar wave of guilt washed over her as she pondered her sins of the past. "*Though they are red like crimson. . .*"

She reached over to turn on the tiny bedside light, then reached for her Bible. She opened to the book of 1 John, chapter two. When she glanced down at the words, amazed at their appropriateness, she knew she must have been guided to this scripture by the Holy Spirit's prompting.

" 'My little children,' " she whispered, " 'these things I write to you, so that you may not sin. And if anyone sins, we have an Advocate with the Father, Jesus Christ the righteous. And He Himself is the propitiation for our sins, and not for ours only but also for the whole world.'"

She read the words over again, letting them sink into her spirit. "'*My little children. . .*'"

The Lord was calling her His child. And tonight, with her past so clearly staring her in the face, she felt a bit like a child, caught in her own actions.

And yet. . .

The Lord had already done a work in her life, had already dealt with so much. Hadn't He?

She checked her heart to see if there was something left undone, some small area she hadn't given over completely to Him.

"Oh Lord," she prayed in a near-silent whisper, "I've been afraid to give you my lingering guilt over not reaching Chris with the news. I could have done more, Lord. I should have tried harder."

She looked at the words once again, allowing them to minister to her. "Thank You, Father, for sending Your Son, Jesus as an atonement for my sins. Thank You for washing me white as snow. And thank You for this precious child of mine." She reached out once more to run her hand across Lorelei's back, and felt a wave of emotion run through her. "Thank You for the blessing she has been to me, and thank You that her future is blessed. Keep her in the palm of Your hand, Father."

Immediately, she felt the Lord's presence as He wrapped His arms around her. She sensed His forgiveness and His peace. Right away, a new burst of energy sent her prayer sailing forward.

"Lord, I know Your Word says You make all things new. That's what I'm asking for tonight. Make things new. Give us a fresh start. Give Chris a desire for his daughter. Give me a. . ."

She wasn't sure what to pray next. A second chance with the man she loved? Did she deserve such a thing? Did she even *want* such a thing?

A muffled ring drew her attention from the other room. Her cell phone? Who would be calling this late?

She tiptoed down the hallway into the living room, where she fetched her phone from her purse. An unfamiliar number lit the screen. She answered hesitantly. "Hello?"

"Hey." Chris's voice greeted her. At once, her heart flew to her throat. "I had to talk to you," he said.

"I'm so glad you called," she confessed. "I couldn't sleep."

"Me neither."

For a moment, neither of them said anything. Adrianne finally broke the silence. "I was just praying."

"Me, too."

More silence.

"I, um. . ." She fought to get the words out. "Chris, I'm so sorry about everything. I don't know if I can ever tell you how sorry I am. You don't know how much I wish I could just go back eight years and do all of this over. I'd change so many things. I promise I would."

"Me, too. This is really all my fault. I'm the one who, who. . ." His voice trailed off.

Adrianne came up with a plan and voiced it right away. "Let's make a deal. No looking back."

He paused a moment before offering up a hesitant "Okay."

"It won't do any good, anyway. And besides, we have to think about where we are. Right now."

There was an undeniable weariness to his voice as he responded. "I've been thinking about it. All night. Needless to say, I don't think I'll be sleeping."

"You have to. You're in a wedding tomorrow."

"Oh, the wedding." He changed gears. "You're coming, right? I really want you to."

"But they hardly know me."

"They know me," he explained. "And that's enough. Besides, Julie sounded pretty insistent."

"I don't know, Chris. I just don't think I could handle it right now. And besides, I've got Lorelei."

"Bring her. Julie said you could bring a guest, right?"

"Chris."

"Seriously." His voice intensified. "Bring her. I know that Stephen and Julie would love it. The wedding is going to be at Christ Church at two o'clock. Do you know where that is?"

"Do I know where that is?" She couldn't help but laugh. "I'm addicted to historic Philly, Chris, you know that. And it just so happens that Ben Franklin attended Christ Church. So did Betsy Ross. And a host of other famous Americans."

"Well then. . ." She could hear the weight lift from his voice as he carried on. "I'm sure they would want you to spend your Saturday afternoon at the place where they were inspired with some of the ideas that made this country what it is today. And besides"—his voice faded a bit—"*this* famous American wants you there. Please?"

A sigh rose up from the back of her throat. How could she resist an invitation like that? "Christ Church at two. I'll think about it."

He whispered a soft "Okay," followed by, "Good night," and then ended the call.

Adrianne clicked the phone shut and made her way back down the darkened hallway into the bedroom. As she slipped beneath the covers, Lorelei rolled over, eyes wide open. Her words very nearly knocked Adrianne clean out of the bed.

"See, Mom," the youngster said with a giggle, "I *told* you he liked you."

✿

"Are you okay, Chris?" Stephen's voice shattered the darkness as Chris entered the hotel room, cell phone in hand.

"Oh, I didn't mean to wake you. I got back to the hotel a long time ago, but was restless, so I went for a walk."

"In the middle of the night?" Stephen flipped on the lamp and sat up in bed.

"Yeah. Then I sat in the lobby long enough to work up the courage to call Adrianne."

Stephen shook his head. "I've been worried about you. When you didn't come back, I didn't know what to think."

"Ah. Well, I didn't mean to worry you, especially not tonight. You've got a big day tomorrow."

Stephen gave him a pensive look. "Big day or not, I've got plenty of time to talk if you need to. And I'm pretty sure you need to. It's written all over your face."

"Oh?" Chris sat on the edge of his bed and looked across the room at his friend. "You think you know me pretty well, don't you?"

"I do."

"Hmm." He wondered what Stephen would say if he told him everything he'd learned tonight. Might be pretty eye-opening.

"So. . ."

Chris just shook his head and didn't respond. "If I get started now, it's going to be a long night." He glanced at the clock. 2:16. Yikes. "It's already been a long night."

"I don't care how long it takes." Stephen crossed his arms and turned to face him. "So you might as well dive in."

"Right." Just a moment or two of silence was all it took. Then, like a flood, the story poured out. Chris felt a huge sense of relief as he told Stephen the details—right down to the most important one. To his credit, Stephen didn't respond, not vocally anyway. His wide-eyed expression at the news of

Lorelei spoke volumes, though.

As he wrapped up the story, Chris opened himself up to his best friend's counsel. He listened as Stephen shared his thoughts, his opinions. And he listened even more intently as his friend—now more serious than he'd ever known him to be—took the time to pray. Aloud. At length. Chris reveled in the fact that the Lord had sent him someone to share this burden.

Somewhere around three thirty, Stephen turned off the light and rolled over. Chris changed out of his clothes and slipped into his bed, unable to fight the weariness any longer. He prayed at length, then, somewhere in the shadows of the night, gave himself over to the exhaustion.

ten

Chris woke up early, in spite of his rough night. He glanced over at Stephen, who snored soundly in the bed next to his. Unable to fall back to sleep, Chris finally rose and slipped on his clothes. Moments later, he found himself walking the beautiful historic streets of downtown Philadelphia, enjoying the solitude of a Saturday morning in blissful silence.

He had to give himself time to think, time to work out a plan of some sort. His mind wouldn't be silenced. As he made his way toward Independence National Park, he breathed in the crisp autumn air and contemplated the overwhelming beauty of the early-morning sun against the red and gold leaves.

He stopped to pick one up, staring at it momentarily. Its changes seemed to signify the transformation in his life. His past seemed as stained as this deep red leaf, but his present, and indeed, his future, could be filled with God's redemptive power, couldn't it? One season had ended, but another one—a fresh one—had begun.

On he walked, finding the city eerily quiet this weekend morning. Soon, he imagined, the tourists would flood the place, in search of the Liberty Bell. Soon the museum would open.

The museum.

Every time he thought about Adrianne's job at the museum, his heart twisted. He couldn't imagine taking her away from the work she loved so much. Besides, she probably wouldn't be interested in the kind of life he lived out on the mission field. How could she be, when she had already settled into a life that brought her such joy?

Stop thinking like that. Just because you have a daughter in common doesn't mean she's ready to be your wife.

Still his mind would not rest. Even if Adrianne married him, agreed to go with him, how would she feel about bringing Lorelei along? Could he justify taking her out of school, away from her friends, her grandparents?

Instantly, Chris's heart began to break. It seemed there was no solution to this problem. *Lord, You know my heart. I'm a missionary. I want to—need to—reach out to people. But right now, I'm so confused. I feel so lost. I thought I had already dealt with all of the forgiveness issues in my life, but here we are again, facing new ones.*

Guilt washed over him afresh, and the deep red leaf in his hand began to tremble, as if in response. He stared at it, transfixed, thinking all the while about his sins, his flaws. How they had come round to meet him once again.

"Though they are red like crimson. . ."

The familiar scripture played out in his mind, though he couldn't imagine where it had come from.

"Though they are red like crimson, they shall be as wool."

He tossed the leaf toward the ground, but the morning breeze picked it up and danced it across the park. Chris watched it, wondering if it would find a home. At last, it came to land on a concrete bench. Still, it seemed unsettled, as if the next brisk wind would pick it up and take it on to another place.

In some ways, his life was like that. He had known the freedom of bouncing from place to place, going wherever he liked. Doing whatever he liked. He'd never really settled down. Not really.

Settling down.

He pondered the words as he started walking again. What would it be like to stay in one place, to own a home? To kiss his wife each morning and tuck his daughter into bed each night? To attend PTA meetings and slip coins under pillows when loose teeth wiggled free? To dance around the living room with his little girl in his arms? To tell her stories about her grandfather, a man she'd never met?

A little shiver ran down Chris's spine as the early morning breeze brought on a chill. Could he—would he—learn to love such a life? Or would he resent it?

His mind traveled again to the tropical jungles of Nicaragua. In his mind's eye, he could see his coworker, David, hammering nails into a church beam. He could see his good friend, Pastor Alejandro, working with machete in hand to clear the weeds so that they could begin their work on a new water well. Dozens of people gathered around, eager to help. The children, their wide brown eyes, smiling, grabbing hold of his hand, calling out, "Mister, Mister!"

Immediately an ache filled Chris's heart. *Lord, help me through this. I don't have a clue which way to turn. I'm going to need Your direction, maybe more than ever before. I'm so. . .clueless.*

In that moment, a picture of Lorelei's cherub-like face flashed before him like a clip from a movie. Her dimples. Her green eyes, a mirror image of his own. Her soft brown hair, familiar in color and form. Her adorable upturned nose, much like her mama's.

Her mama's.

Chris's heart swelled at the thought of Adrianne as a mother. She seemed to take to the task quite easily. He tried to imagine what her life must be like, balancing a child and a job. He tried to picture what it must be like in the mornings as the two girls—*his* two girls—prepared for the day.

What was it like, he wondered, on those mornings when

Adrianne simply didn't feel like getting out of bed and going to work? Who did she talk to on those days when she felt lonely or confused? Who did she turn to for comfort when Lorelei was sick, or acting up, even?

Did Adrianne have someone in her life to love? Someone with whom she could share her hopes and dreams?

Right away, Chris's heart ached. *I would have been there for her, if I had known. I would have.*

I still could be.

But how?

He sat on the bench, deep in thought for some time. Finally, the park began to fill with tourists, just as he'd predicted. He looked across the park at a little boy and his mother, walking hand in hand. The youngster tugged at his mom's fingers with one hand and pointed at the Liberty Bell with the other.

"Look, Mama! Look!"

"I see, I see." She purchased a ticket and took her place in the now growing line in front of the familiar landmark.

Chris glanced down at his watch: 10:45. Stephen would be looking for him soon. They had a big day ahead.

As he stood to begin the trip back to the hotel, Chris couldn't seem to take his eyes off of the little boy's mother. *She was born for this.*

Just like Adrianne. *She* was born for the role she now played, he had to acknowledge. Born to be a parent.

Born to be a parent.

With a seven-year-old daughter, *he* was surely born to be a parent, too. And it was about time he started acting like one.

&

Adrianne awoke with a splitting headache. She rolled over in the bed to find Lorelei had already awakened. From the living room, she could hear the strains of a familiar cartoon theme song.

"Ah. She's watching TV."

Adrianne yawned and stretched, wishing she could sleep just a bit longer. She glanced over at the clock and groaned. "No way. Ten fifty?" How in the world could she have slept so late?

On the other hand, she hadn't actually fallen asleep until sometime after four. No wonder she'd slept in.

About that time, Adrianne heard noises coming from the kitchen. "Oh no. Not that."

She bounded from her bed and sprinted down the hallway. As she turned into the kitchen, she caught Lorelei with a fork in hand, trying to pry an overcooked pastry from the toaster.

"No, Lorelei. Don't do that." She grabbed the fork from her daughter's hand, all the while trying not to overreact.

"It's stuck." Lorelei's pouty face would have been cute under other circumstances.

"I know." Adrianne unplugged the toaster, turned it upside down, and weaseled the pastry out. "But you can't put something metal down inside the toaster. You could have been electrocuted. It's very dangerous."

"I didn't know." Lorelei reached to grab the burnt pastry and popped a piece in her mouth.

"Don't eat that," Adrianne scolded.

Lorelei spoke around the mouthful of food. "But I want it."

"I'm going to make a really special breakfast."

"Mmm. What?"

"How about. . ." She thought for a minute. "Chocolate chip pancakes?"

"Yummy!" Lorelei squealed. She opened the pantry door and tossed the pastry in the trash. "I love your pancakes." Immediately, the youngster reached up to the shelf that housed the pancake mix. After that, she opened the refrigerator door and pulled out the carton of eggs. She then snatched the jug of milk in hand and placed it on the kitchen counter.

"Goodness," Adrianne said with a smile. "You've already done half the work. Why don't you just make the pancakes, too?"

"I'll help." Lorelei reached into a drawer in the refrigerator for the bag of chocolate chips. "I like to cook. Grandma says I'm good at it."

"I'm glad one of us is." Adrianne couldn't help but sigh.

"It's okay, Mom." Lorelei turned to give her a more-than-serious face. "Chris will still like you, even if your cooking is bad."

Adrianne turned to face her daughter. Standing there with that hopeful look in her eyes, Lorelei looked, for all the world, like her father.

"Excuse me? Who said anything about Chris?" Adrianne tried to hide the smile from her face, but it would not be squelched. Instead, the more she thought about him, the broader it grew.

"He likes you, he likes you." Lorelei whispered the words over and over as she cracked two eggs into a large mixing bowl. Then she turned to face her mother head-on, startling her with her next words. "And you like him, too!"

eleven

"How do I look?" Stephen fidgeted with his tie and Chris reached over to help him straighten it. No matter how hard he tried, he couldn't get the crazy thing to cooperate.

"You look like a happy man." Chris glanced down at his watch. "A man who's getting married in less than ten minutes."

Stephen glanced in the mirror one last time, checking his hair. "I can't believe it." He turned back to face Chris. "Everyone tells you the whole wedding-day thing is kind of surreal, and they're right. It's weird, almost like it's happening to someone else, not me." His face broadened in a smile. "Are you sure *you're* not getting married today instead of me?"

"Um, no." Chris shook his head. "I'm pretty sure I'd remember that." His heart wrenched as the words were spoken. Whether he wanted to admit it or not, he wished he could trade places with Stephen. His thoughts shifted at once to Adrianne. And Lorelei. *His* Lorelei.

Stephen must have taken note of his change of mood. "You doing okay?" He slipped an arm around Chris's shoulders in a show of support.

Chris looked up, embarrassed. "Oh. Yeah. Just thinking."

"You won't have to think long on this one, I'd guess. I've known you for years, and one thing is for sure—you're a man who finishes well, Chris Bradley." Stephen patted him on the back, then once again turned his attention to his tie.

You're a man who finishes well.

Why did the words shake him to the core? Ah. Because he

wanted it so badly, probably. He wanted to finish well, wanted to make up for the mistakes of the past.

Something across the room caught his eye. He walked over to a large glass case and glanced down at the open Bible inside. "Hey, did you notice this?" he asked.

Stephen joined him, looking down at the leather-bound Bible. "Nope. Man, that thing is old. I wonder if it. . . You don't suppose it dates all the way back to the founding of the church, do you?"

Chris shrugged. "I don't know. But it's amazing. Look at the lettering."

"Wow."

They stared in silence for a moment and Chris pondered the possibility that many great men of faith—possibly even America's founding fathers—might have read from this same book throughout the generations.

As Stephen turned back to finish getting ready for the ceremony, Chris noticed for the first time that the King James Bible was opened to the twelfth chapter of Hebrews.

" 'Wherefore seeing we also are compassed about with so great a cloud of witnesses,' " he read aloud, " 'let us lay aside every weight, and the sin which doth so easily beset us, and let us run with patience the race that is set before us, looking unto Jesus the author and finisher of our faith; who for the joy that was set before him endured the cross, despising the shame, and is set down at the right hand of the throne of God.' "

"Amen," Stephen said when he finished. "Great scripture to share with a man on his wedding day—when he feels like the whole world is out there, in front of him—a race waiting to be run." He gave a knowing smile.

Chris sighed. "Great scripture to read on a day when I'm feeling like my past is catching up with me."

"Is that how you feel?" Stephen slipped an arm around his

shoulder. "Like a kid who's been caught doing something he shouldn't have been?"

"A little," Chris acknowledged. "But it's such a strange mixture of feelings. I'm so excited about Lorelei. I don't even know if I can explain how excited. And Adrianne. . ." The edges of his lips turned up as he thought about her.

"You still care for her, don't you?"

Chris nodded, and forced back the lump in his throat. "That's the strange part. I do. I mean, I thought I'd given the whole thing over to the Lord years ago. But I still care about her. Very much."

"I'd say it's because you gave it over to the Lord that you still have the capacity to care," Stephen added. "But then again, you probably already knew that." He gave him a friendly slap on the back, and then turned his attention back to his tie. "Could you help me with this?"

"Oh, of course." Chris jumped back into best-man gear, finally getting the wayward tie in place. Moments later, the other groomsmen entered the room with guilty looks on their faces.

"Where have you guys been?" Stephen gave his tie a final pat and turned to face his friends.

"Oh, we, uh. . ." George Ferguson gave a shrug. "We had to talk to a man about a horse."

"Sure you did." Stephen's eyes flashed a warning. "What were you up to?"

"Nothing." Phil Sanders, the younger of the two, glanced in the mirror, then reached for a comb. "Nothing you need to worry about, anyway."

"If you were messing with my car. . . ," Stephen started.

George's face gave away their prank before he spoke. "Who said anything about your car?"

"I told you guys not to do it. Wedding or no wedding."

Chris looked back and forth between George and Phil. Neither said a word, but they had clearly "done the deed," as it were.

At that moment, Stephen's father entered the room, carrying boutonnieres. "The wedding planner is in over her head with the bridesmaids," he explained. "So she asked me if I could make sure these made it into the right hands."

All of the guys scrambled, trying to figure out how to fasten the fall-colored flowers onto their tuxedo jackets. A knock on the door interrupted their frenzy.

"Nearly ready?" The minister, a pleasant-looking fellow, asked as he entered the room. "The organist has just started the Brandenburg Concerto and that's our cue. All of the guests are seated." He glanced to his right, noted Stephen struggling with the boutonniere, and came to the rescue. "Let me get this for you. I've become something of an expert over the years."

"Thanks, Rev. Stone." The color seemed to drain from Stephen's face even as he spoke the words.

"Are you okay, man?" Chris asked.

"Yeah. Just feeling a little nauseous."

Rev. Stone finished with the boutonniere, and then went on to offer a bit of advice. "Don't lock your knees."

"I beg your pardon?" Stephen's brow wrinkled.

"When you get out there in front of the crowd, don't lock your knees. Keep them slightly bent." The older man's face softened slightly as he demonstrated the proper stance. "It's been my experience that we lose a lot of grooms when they lock their knees."

"Ah."

"And deep breaths, young man." He faced Stephen. "Remember, it's not about the ceremony. It's about the marriage."

Chris couldn't help but laugh as Stephen took several slow,

deep breaths. *He really is nervous.*

"Here we go." Rev. Stone led the way to the door that opened into the large, formal sanctuary. Stephen trailed him, with Chris following along like a puppy on his heels. George and Phil fell into place behind Chris, and within minutes they were standing at the front of the crowd.

As he looked around the magnificent room with its rich historical elements, Chris thought about what Adrianne had said on the phone. *"Ben Franklin attended Christ Church. So did Betsy Ross."* He gaze shifted upward, to the large white balconies and arched windows. They were amazing, really, though noticeably different from the churches he'd helped build in Nicaragua. There they were lucky to have openings for windows. No glass at all.

Yes, this place was great. And how remarkable, to consider the countless historic things that had surely happened here. Great men and women of faith had stood in this very spot, perhaps preached in this very place.

This is a room where amazing things have happened, I feel sure of it. In this room, the Lord has spoken to many of our forefathers.

"Lord," the word came out as the faintest of whispers, "speak to me. Here, in this place. Speak to me. Show me Your will."

Chris's eyes were immediately drawn to the crowd. Had Adrianne and Lorelei come? Were they here?

No, he saw no sign of them. Keen disappointment set in, but it was short-lived. *Stay focused. You're here for Stephen and Julie.*

A change in music signaled the entrance of the bridesmaids. One by one, they entered the room to the familiar strain of Pachelbel's Canon in D. They joined the men at the front, and then the moment arrived. The "Bridal March" began, and the crowd rose to its feet.

As soon as the doors opened and Julie—radiant in white satin—walked in on her father's arm, Chris's attention shifted to Stephen. *What does it feel like, to watch the woman you love walking up the aisle? Is your heart so full you can hardly stand it? Are you a nervous wreck?*

The bride literally glowed with joy as she approached and took Stephen's hand. Together, they entered the altar area. Chris felt the sting of tears as he turned with the others to face the minister. Just as he did, however, something at the back of the room caught his eye. Someone—rather, a couple of someones—slipped in the back door unnoticed. Unnoticed by anyone other than himself, anyway.

Right away, his heart soared. *They're here. My daughter and my. . .*

"We've come here this day to unite this man and this woman in holy matrimony." The minister's words rang out across the sanctuary, creating a near hollow sound against the marble floor and the wooden pews. "Marriage is an honorable estate, and not to be entered into lightly. . . ." He continued on with his opening remarks, but Chris found it difficult to focus, at least on Stephen and Julie. No, he saw himself standing in their spot. With Adrianne at his side.

&

"Mom, look!"

Adrianne glanced over at Lorelei and shushed her.

"But, Mom"—Lorelei pointed at the flower girl, a pretty little thing with blonde ringlets and a beautiful white dress— "I've never been a flower girl."

Right away, Adrianne's finger went to her lips. "We have to be quiet," she whispered. "We can talk about it afterward." She tried to focus on the ceremony, but found her gaze shifting to Chris. He looked remarkable in his black tuxedo. Breathtaking, actually.

Don't do that. Pay attention.

The wedding couple exchanged vows, hand in hand, love pouring from their eyes.

What would it feel like, to stand up there? What would I be thinking. . .doing?

Her gaze shifted to the large columns to her right and left, then lifted to the carved balconies on the second floor. The chandelier overhead cast a warm glow on the room, reminding her of days gone by. Though not as ornate as some of the other churches in the historic district, this one still captivated her more than any of the others. Probably because Ben Franklin had attended church here. Perhaps sitting in this very pew. Just the idea of it put goose bumps on her arms. *How is it that I can be so intrigued with someone from history?*

"*Because he changed lives. He left a legacy.*"

The words nearly rocked her off the pew. Yes, he and the other founding fathers had certainly left a legacy.

And that's exactly what she wanted to do, too.

Familiar words from the minister directed her attention back up to the front of the sanctuary. "You may now kiss the bride."

Lorelei's eyes grew large as Stephen and Julie kissed. "You're going to get married someday, too, Mom. And you'll get kissed, don't worry." Her forced whisper was a little too loud, catching the attention of the elderly lady who sat in front of them. The somewhat matronly looking woman turned with a scolding look on her face.

Adrianne mouthed *I'm sorry*, then turned her attention back to the minister's closing remarks, hoping Lorelei would keep her thoughts to herself.

No such luck.

"Look, Mom!" Her daughter pointed at Chris as he made his way down the aisle, along with others in the wedding party. "I see Chris."

"Yes." Adrianne couldn't hide her smile.

"He looks handsome, just like Prince Charming. See, I *told* you!"

"Lorelei," Adrianne whispered the words, but let her eyes do the begging, "please don't. Please."

Thankfully, the joyous strains of Vivaldi's "Four Seasons" theme drowned out the youngster's voice.

Almost.

Lorelei's jovial attitude quickly faded as she noticed the pretty bridesmaid on Chris's arm. She turned to face her mother, pain registering in her eyes. "Is that his *girlfriend*?"

"Please—lower—your—voice." Adrianne mouthed the words—slowly, succinctly.

Lorelei seemed to pay her no mind at all. Instead, she took advantage of his nearness to give him a little wave.

Adrianne buried her head in her hands and wondered if she would ever get over the embarrassment of this afternoon as long as she lived.

She lifted her gaze just as Prince Charming walked by, tuxedo shimmering under the chandelier overhead.

Chris nodded their way and even gave Lorelei a wink. Then he turned his gaze to Adrianne. The love that showed in his eyes nearly caused her to stop breathing altogether, and for a moment—just a moment—she contemplated tossing a glass slipper his way.

twelve

"What are you doing, Mom?"

Adrianne dug around in her purse for pennies, finally capturing a few. "Come with me," she said, taking Lorelei by the hand. "I have something to show you."

Together, they scooted around the wedding party at the front of Christ Church and walked around to the old burial ground nearby.

"A cemetery?" Lorelei's eyes widened. "I don't want to go in there."

"Don't worry, we're not." Adrianne handed her the pennies, then pointed out one of the large, flat gravesites several yards away. "That's where Ben Franklin is buried, that gravestone right there."

"Ooh." A sound of admiration rose from her daughter's lips. "Why are there pennies all over it?"

"Well," Adrianne explained, "Ben always had a saying, 'A penny saved is a penny earned.' He's remembered for witty things like that. So tourists come by here and toss pennies. It's a tradition. People have been doing it for hundreds of years. And I thought you might like to try. But you have to do it from outside the fence."

"Cool." Lorelei took aim, then tossed the first penny. It missed by about three feet. She turned back to her mother with a pout.

"Try the other one."

The youngster tried again. This time, the penny came within inches. "Do you have more, Mom?"

Adrianne reached inside her purse once again. "I don't think so. But you were close, anyway."

"I have a penny."

They turned quickly as Chris's voice seemed to sweep over them from behind. He stood closer than her own breath, his brilliant green eyes dancing in the afternoon sunlight.

"I. . .I thought you were busy having photos done," she explained. "And I wanted to show Lorelei something from our history." *Something from our history. Hmm. Probably should have worded that differently.*

He held up a copper penny between his thumb and fore-finger and smiled. "Want to include me?"

His words caused her hands to tremble. Yes, she wanted to include him. In her life. In her daughter's life. In her decisions, her hopes, her dreams, her future. Everything.

Lorelei reached up to snatch the penny from his hand. "Can I try again?" she asked.

"You may."

This time she tossed the coin and it landed in the center of the gravestone. "I did it!" She jumped up and down, excitement oozing from every pore.

"You did it." Adrianne and Chris spoke in unison, then turned in laughter, suddenly finding themselves face-to-face.

Adrianne felt his breath warm on her cheek, and for a moment thought of pulling away. But something inside her wouldn't allow it. Instead, she remained still as he leaned in close. Her eyes closed instinctively. She remembered the taste of his lips against hers. Eight years might have passed, but some things would never be forgotten.

"Chris, are you ready to go?" Stephen's voice rang out from around the corner, and Adrianne's heart leaped into her throat as Chris pulled away quite suddenly.

"Mom?" Lorelei grabbed her hand and stared up, eyes blazing

with laughter. "See, I *told* you."

"Told you what?" Chris asked, his cheeks flushed pink.

"I *told* you he would kiss you."

Adrianne looked up in embarrassment, only to find Chris's beautiful green eyes riveted on hers. She did her best to shift gears, feeling a little foolish for giving away her feelings in front of her daughter. "Wh–who said anything about kissing?"

Chris gave her a look that voiced his opinion on the matter. She could read the *"I did"* in his expression.

As if in response, Lorelei grabbed their hands and pressed them together. Then, with a smile on her face, she led the way to the front of the church to meet the others.

❧

Chris's heart sang all the way to the wedding reception. He had seen the look in Adrianne's eyes. She still loved him, in spite of everything. And he loved her, too. With every fiber of his being.

And Lorelei. . .

He couldn't help but wonder at the youngster's tenacity—or her matchmaking skills. Clearly, she wanted to see the two of them together.

For obvious reason, he chided himself. *Of course she wants to see us together. She's been without a father all of her life.*

He pushed aside the feelings of guilt that suddenly rose to the surface and focused on the activities ahead. Any moment now, he would arrive with the rest of the bridal party at the reception hall, where they would make a grand entrance. Hopefully, Adrianne and Lorelei would stay for a while, until his duties as best man had ended. He had so much to say to her, so much to share.

Within moments, Chris and the others entered the lavish Ballroom at the Ben—and found the room filled with cheering wedding guests. The music started right away and the bride and groom headed off to the dance floor for their first dance as a married couple.

Chris stood off to the side, scoping out the room. *Ah. There they are.* Adrianne and Lorelei—his girls—sat at a table nearby. They smiled his way, and Lorelei waved in excitement. He made his way through the crowd toward them.

"This place is great, don't you think?" Adrianne gestured around the room.

For some reason, he couldn't focus on the room, only her rich brown eyes as they danced in excitement.

"Beautiful," he said with a hint of a smile rising to his lips.

"Those chandeliers are absolutely exquisite."

"Exquisite," he echoed, still paying no attention whatsoever to the room.

"And the gold trim on those archways is unbelievable."

"Unbelievable."

Adrianne looked Chris's way and caught his meaning. Her face reddened. A feeling of warmth rushed over him, and he wanted to sweep her into his arms again. Instead, Lorelei caught his attention, pointing at the couple on the dance floor.

"She looks like Cinderella, Mom."

"Yes, she does." Adrianne nodded. "And look who she's dancing with—Prince Charming."

"No she's not." Lorelei looked up at Chris with a shy face, and he tried to decipher her meaning.

Just then, the music ended and the DJ announced the opening of the buffet line. Lorelei tipped her face upward and grinned. "Food, Mom!"

Adrianne seemed to snap out of her somewhat dreamy state, looking over at Chris with a more practical look on her face. "I—I don't want to keep you from your friends. We'll just sit over here. . ."

Chris let out a sigh. "I guess I do need to sit at the head table with the wedding party. I'm still officially on the clock."

"Always a groomsman. . ." Adrianne started, then slapped her hand over her mouth. "Oh, I'm so sorry. That was totally inappropriate."

"Nah." He grinned. "I'm used to it."

Always a groomsman. But maybe not for long.

The rest of the evening played out just as he'd hoped it would. Though dedicated to his best friend, he managed to snatch some well-deserved moments with Adrianne and Lorelei. And at one point, well after offering the toast, he even managed to ask her to dance. Lorelei, not Adrianne.

The youngster's face lit with excitement as she took him by the hand and they walked to the dance floor together.

As Chris circled around with his daughter's hand clutched in his, tears came. He couldn't control them. *This is my first father-daughter dance. But it won't be my last.*

Through the tears, he glanced over at Adrianne, who sat alone at the table, eyes glistening.

When I'm done, Adrianne Russo, he vowed, *you're next. And this time, I'm not going to let you get away.*

thirteen

Adrianne looked up as Lorelei's happy-go-lucky voice rang out above the crowd of people in the fellowship hall.

"I'm going to kids' church, Mom!"

Adrianne turned her attention away from Mrs. Norris, one of the members of her church, to focus on her daughter. She turned back to the older woman with a smile. "Excuse me. Looks like I'm needed."

She finally caught up with her daughter. Taking her by the arm, she asked, "Hey, what's your hurry?"

"I don't want them to start without me."

Adrianne glanced at her watch: 9:15. "Yikes. I didn't know it was this late." Seemed like the whole morning had been a bit "off," what with getting so little sleep last night. Then again, who could sleep, with the crystal-clear memory of Chris wrapping her in his arms for a turn around the dance floor?

"Mom, are you coming?" Lorelei's voice jarred Adrianne back to the present. Together, they made their way through the throng of people to the children's church room. All along the way, familiar faces greeted her. When they arrived, Adrianne stopped for a short chat with Jacquie Levron, director of the children's ministry.

"Are you ready for tonight?" she asked.

Jacquie nodded, but her expression carried a bit of concern. "Pretty much. Some of the kids haven't memorized their lines yet, and Phillip Johnson has strep throat, but you know what they say. . ."

"The show must go on." The two women spoke in unison.

Adrianne couldn't help but laugh. "So, tell me." She lowered her voice a bit. "How do you think Lorelei is doing? She's been practicing every day."

"Oh, Adrianne." Jacquie's voice lit up. "That girl of yours is amazing. Of course, she has a voice like an angel. I've told you that before. But there's something more to it than that. When Lorelei sings. . ." Jacquie shook her head, apparently trying to find the right words, "When Lorelei sings, there's an anointing on her. You can feel the presence of God."

Goose bumps rippled down Adrianne's arms as she nodded in response. "I'm her mom," she acknowledged, "so I thought it was just me—thought I was just reading too much into it."

Jacquie's smiled broadened. "No, you're not reading too much into it. That girl was born to sing. And I'm so glad to have her in our church. Not just because she's talented, Adrianne." Her voice took on a more serious tone. "But because she's a good girl. Genuine. Her walk with the Lord is evident. And it's so pure."

"It's so pure."

Adrianne brushed back the tears as she turned to leave the room. *Lord, how is it possible? This child, born out of my sin, is as pure as the driven snow. She's such a blessing to me, such a joy. What would I have done without her?*

She shifted her thoughts as she headed into the sanctuary. Her parents would be waiting. Probably in the fourth row on the left, as usual. Yep. There they were.

"G'morning, baby. How are you?" Her mother reached over to wrap her in a warm embrace.

Adrianne knew that, no matter how long she lived, she would always be referred to as her mother's baby. She also knew that she loved the reference, for it implied innocence. Purity.

There's that word again.

Snapping back to her senses, Adrianne answered her mother's question. "I'm great. Lorelei and I went to the wedding yesterday."

"Tell me all about it." Her mom ushered her to a seat and Adrianne quickly relayed the whole story—everything from the beautiful ceremony, to the dance she and Chris had shared at the end of the night.

Her father listened in without saying a word, but she observed the look in his eye when she reached the part of the story where Chris had swept Lorelei into his arms for a father-daughter dance.

"He's a good man, Adrianne." Her dad gave a nod. "But I think you already knew that."

"Yes."

Chris Bradley had always been a good man—a man after God's own heart. Yes, he had made mistakes. They both had. But God had restored them, and that meant the past was truly in the past.

The worship team began to play a familiar praise and worship song, and the congregation stood. As Adrianne sang, her heart soared. *Lord, You're so good to me.* A few moments later, the familiar strains of a slower worship song began, a song Adrianne had always loved. She sensed God's overwhelming presence, and closed her eyes, ready to let Him minister to her in any way He pleased.

"See, child. Do you see how much I love you?"

The tears came at once. She didn't even bother to wipe them away.

" 'Though your sins are like scarlet. . . ,' " she whispered.

"I've erased those sins, My daughter. I've forgiven and forgotten, as far as the east is from the west."

" 'Though they are red like crimson. . .' "

"The only crimson I see is the precious blood of My Son, who takes away the sins of the world."

Adrianne drew in a deep breath and brushed the tears away.

"Adrianne?" Her father leaned over with a soft whisper, concern registering in his eyes. "Everything okay?"

She took him by the hand and mouthed the words *Yes. Very okay.*

He gave her fingers a little squeeze, then leaned over to plant a kiss on her forehead. In that moment, a thousand feelings washed over her at once. Poor Lorelei had never known the love of a father's kiss pressed upon her brow. She'd never experienced the comfort of a gentle squeeze of a daddy's hand, or the wink of his eye.

Thank You, God, for my father. Thank You for giving me such an idyllic family life. I don't know what I've ever done to deserve it. . .to deserve him.

As if he'd read her thoughts, her father turned and gave a wink. She nodded his way, then shifted her attention to the front of the room and focused on the pastor. He opened the message with a scripture from the Psalms, one of Adrianne's favorites.

" 'As far as the east is from the west,' " he read, " 'so far has He removed our transgressions from us.' " The pastor forged ahead, his words laced with excitement. "I had another message planned for today," he explained, "but at the prompting of the Holy Spirit, I've gone a different direction. I've titled this morning's message, 'From the East to the West.' "

He went on to share one of the most amazing sermons Adrianne had ever heard on forgiveness, honing in on God's ability to forget, as well as forgive.

Oh, if only I could forget! If only I could wipe away all traces of my past.

"Turn with me in your Bibles to the book of Psalms, chapter 32," Pastor Monahan said.

Adrianne turned to the passage and the pastor began to read aloud, starting in the first verse.

" 'Blessed is he whose transgression is forgiven, whose sin is covered. Blessed is the man to whom the Lord does not impute iniquity, and in whose spirit there is no deceit.'

"When our sins are forgiven," Pastor Monahan said, "God can't count them against us. And it's clear why, when we turn to the book of Isaiah, chapter 43.

Adrianne flipped through the pages of her Bible until she landed on the chapter in question.

" 'I, even I, am He who blots out your transgressions,'" the pastor read, " 'for My own sake; and I will not remember your sins.' " He looked up at the congregation as he repeated the words, " 'I will not remember your sins.'"

After a slight chuckle, he continued. "We can't seem to forget offenses that others commit against us, whether they happened yesterday or last year. It's so difficult for us to forget, isn't it? And how much harder is it for us to forgive ourselves when we've broken God's heart? Sometimes forgiving ourselves is the hardest thing of all."

Adrianne squirmed a bit, and her father reached over to give her hand a squeeze.

Pastor Monahan's eyes lit with excitement as he spoke. "How ironic is it," he said, "that the Lord loves sinners, but hates sin? How fascinating, that the price to pay for forgiveness is so very high, but that He was willing to pay it? And how amazing, that God doesn't even keep a record—or a transcript—of our sins. He doesn't forgive in part. He forgives completely."

Adrianne listened intently, thankful for the Lord's reminder that she could not only put the past behind her, but that He would remember it no more.

"How do we receive this forgiveness?" Pastor Monahan asked. "When you come to the Lord, truly repentant, and put your trust in the work done on the cross, your sins are washed away. Erased. Doesn't matter how big. Doesn't matter how bad. The blood of Jesus was—and is—sufficient to wash away any trace or stain of sin."

"Any trace of sin." Adrianne whispered the words. '*Though they are red like crimson. . .*'

As the pastor's words flowed forth, Adrianne couldn't help but think the Lord, Himself, had planned this message just for her. She would learn to walk in forgiveness—for her sake, and for her daughter's.

❧

Chris's cell phone rang just as he and the other groomsmen finished up their lunch at the hotel. The sound of Adrianne's voice on the other end brought a smile to his lips right away. He excused himself from the table and took the call outside.

"I'm so glad it's you," he said.

He noticed a bit of hesitation in her voice as she responded, "Yeah. I needed to call. We have a lot to work out."

"Right." He pondered that for a moment. Had she called with a particular plan in mind, or was she as clueless as he was?

"How long are you in town?"

"I leave tomorrow afternoon for Virginia Beach. Then it's back to Managua three days later."

"Oh."

Was that disappointment in her voice? He hoped so, prayed so. "Are you free today at all?"

"Well, I was actually calling with an invitation." Her voice seemed to lift a bit with her next words. "Lorelei is in a play at church tonight. She's singing a couple of solos, actually."

"Ah." He grinned. "She is her mother's daughter, isn't she?"

Adrianne chuckled. "Yeah. But, to be honest, I haven't sung in years."

He couldn't hide the disappointment from his voice as he said, "That's a shame."

"Well," Adrianne continued on, "in all honesty, she's far better than I ever was."

"I doubt that." Chris couldn't remember anything clearer—or purer—than the sound of Adrianne's voice as she sang out to the Lord. He had held on to that memory for eight years now. And her performances back in college had mesmerized plenty of people besides him.

"Well, I guess you're just going to have to come and hear her for yourself. Then you'll know I'm telling the truth."

Chris smiled as he heard the pride in her voice. "Just name the time and place and I'm there."

"I was thinking I could come by and pick you up after I drop off Lorelei for rehearsal. That way, we could spend a little time talking beforehand."

His heart quickened. "S—sounds good. What time will you be here?"

"Five?"

"Five. Okay. Dressy or casual?"

"Casual."

"Casual it is." Chris leaned back against the side of the building and paused a moment before saying the one thing he'd been dying to say since he took her in his arms last night. Finally, the courage gripped him. "Adrianne?"

"Yes?"

"I—I still love you. I do." *More than I can stand to say.*

Her silence seemed to go on an eternity. When she finally did speak, he could hear the emotion in her voice and knew she was crying. "I—I know."

Please say you love me, too. Say it, and I'll know what to do.

"I. . ." Her voice took on a more practical sound. "I'll pick you up at five."

Though he suddenly felt the wind had been knocked out of his sails, Chris managed to eek out a quick good-bye. Then, with his back still pressed firmly to the wall, he closed his eyes and allowed the tears to come.

fourteen

Chris entered the sanctuary of the inner-city church and looked around in amazement. The architecture of the the Freedom Fellowship Church could hardly be compared to the grandeur of Christ Church, but something about this place just felt—right. Good.

"Wow. This is really cool. I've been to a lot of churches, but never seen one converted from a warehouse like this before."

"It's more of a storefront ministry," Adrianne explained. "We do a lot of inner-city outreaches. And we deal with a lot of homeless people, too. I always like to tell people that we're a little different right off the bat so they won't be surprised. Our church has an inner-city 'face,' if that makes sense. Lots of people with lots of issues. New converts, I guess you'd say."

"I understand. They sound a lot like the people I worked with in Nicaragua. People new to the faith, with a lot of things to unravel in their lives. Lots of alcohol problems, especially."

"Same here." She looked at him, eyes wide. "Sounds like we've kind of been working along the same lines all along. Weird, huh?"

"Yeah."

She led the way to the third row of chairs and gestured for him to take a seat. As he did, an older woman leaned over to shake his hand.

"Welcome."

Chris nodded. "Thanks."

"This is Mrs. Norris," Adrianne explained with a nod. "She

heads up our ministry to shut-ins."

"Great to meet you." He flashed a broad smile. Something about the woman reminded him a bit of Alejandro's wife. Her colorful attire, perhaps? Her silver hair swept up in a bun?

"Do you have a child in the play tonight?" Mrs. Norris asked.

Chris's heart almost stopped. Especially when he saw the look that crossed Adrianne's face. If he said no, he'd be lying. If he said yes, the woman would likely ask which child.

"Actually, I've got a—"

Thankfully, the musicians on stage began to play, signaling the beginning of the service. The woman shrugged and took her seat. Chris wiped a bead of sweat from his brow.

"That was a close one," Adrianne whispered.

"Yeah."

At that moment, her parents slipped into their seats next to them. "Sorry we're late," her mother said. "I had a long-distance call from your brother in Kuwait. I finally told him that I had to go, that our little angel was playing the starring role in her first play."

Adrianne smiled in her direction. "It's fine. You didn't miss anything."

Chris made a mental note to ask Adrianne about her brother. *Kuwait. He must be in the military.*

His thought shifted back to the service as the worship leader, a young man in his late twenties perhaps, came to the center of the stage and asked everyone to stand. He led them in three or four worship songs, then turned the service over to the elementary director, whose face shone with excitement.

She introduced the production, and the lights went down. Moments later, a spotlight came up—on his daughter. Center stage. She wore a biblical costume, along with the brightest smile he'd ever seen.

For just a second, Chris was overcome with nerves for her.

No need. She dove into the opening song with great gusto, her beautiful voice ringing out loud and clear. She sang with the joy of a youngster, but the clarity and vocal strength of a grown woman. In fact, she sounded for all the world like her mother, the last time he heard her sing in church. Eight years ago.

Whether he meant to do it or not, Chris could not be sure, but he reached to take Adrianne's hand and gave it a squeeze. She squeezed back, a good sign. He glanced at her out of the corner of his eye. Were those tears?

Yes. She dabbed at her eyes with her other hand, never taking her focus off of the stage. Was she crying because of Lorelei's performance, or had the events of the past few days finally taken their toll? He offered up another gentle squeeze and she responded by gripping his hand.

The play went on, creating both laughter and tears from those watching. Chris couldn't remember ever having so much fun in church. And the fact that his daughter ripped his heart out with her obvious love for the Lord only made the evening more enjoyable.

When the production came to an end, the audience members rose to their feet and applauded. Chris stood, with tears in his eyes, clapping madly. Afterward, once the lights came back on in the auditorium, he caught Lorelei's attention from a distance. She ran all the way from the stage, directly into his outstretched arms.

"Chris! You came!"

He did his best not to let the moisture in his eyes give him away. "I came. And I'm so proud of you."

She wrapped her hands around his neck and gave him a squeeze. "Thank you. It was so fun!" After he put her back down, she pulled at her mother's blouse. "Can we go out for ice cream with everybody else?"

Adrianne looked at Chris with a little shrug. "Several of us like to go out after church on Sunday nights. It's kind of a tradition."

"Will you come, Chris?" Lorelei looked up with a pretend pout, trying to woo him.

"I'd love to. I'm all for tradition." Chris had the oddest feelings run through him as he spoke the words. He was suddenly aware of the time crunch, aware of the fact that he would be leaving tomorrow to return to Virginia Beach, and then on to Nicaragua shortly thereafter. Aware of the fact that he needed to take advantage of every possible moment with Lorelei.

And Adrianne.

He looked over at the beauty on his left. With her dark curls framing the splattering of freckles on her cheeks, she looked like something from a magazine. But there was more to her than physical beauty, for sure. Her inner strength, her passion for life—these were the things that made her the woman she was.

"Do you think it's okay if I go with you two?"

Adrianne's lips curled up a bit as she responded, "Of course."

Right then and there, Chris's heart took flight. Yes, he would go with them. To the moon, if they asked him to.

❧

Adrianne had spent the better part of the performance trying to catch her breath. She couldn't tell which had her more unnerved, Lorelei's amazing performance or the delicious comfort of Chris's hand in her own.

Face it. You're a wreck because you're still in love with him. Something about sitting here in church, with Chris at her side, felt so good, so right.

And yet. . .

The whole thing seemed like a childish dream. In reality, he would leave tomorrow, returning to his work in Central America. Their conversation in the car had revealed that much, though the sadness in his eyes had been evident.

Yes, tomorrow Chris would walk out of her life, just as she had walked out of his all those many years ago. And she and Lorelei would be left alone to fend for themselves. Again.

fifteen

After ordering two banana splits and a small hot fudge sundae, Chris and Adrianne joined a couple of others at a small booth in the back of the ice cream parlor. All along the way, he watched her as she interacted with others, fascinating thoughts taking hold. *She's just as social as she ever was. And her face still lights up like a maraschino cherry when she orders a banana split.* Some things really didn't change with time.

"Chris, this is our pastor, Jake Monahan." Adrianne made the introductions with a smile on her face.

Clearly, she admired her pastor. Chris reached out to shake the man's hand. "Nice to meet you."

Jake introduced his wife, Katelyn, whose smile broadened as her gaze traveled back and forth between Chris and Adrianne.

"Any friend of Adrianne's is a friend of ours," she said with a somewhat mischievous grin. "Are you from Philly?"

"No. Just here for a wedding." Chris pondered those words as soon as he said them. This trip to Philadelphia might have started out as a simple wedding trip, but had rapidly morphed into something else altogether.

Lorelei appeared at the table, licking her lips as she gazed at the hot fudge sundae. "Is that mine?" she asked.

"It is." Adrianne passed it her way. "But you owe Mr. Bradley a thank-you. He was kind enough to treat us tonight."

"Thank you, thank you!" She took the sundae and, after asking her mother's permission, sat at the next table with several of her friends.

Chris turned his attention back to Adrianne as she continued on with the introductions. "Chris and I have been good friends since college. He's in missions work," she explained to the pastor and his wife. "Foreign missions, I mean."

Pastor Monahan's face lit up immediately. "Really? Where?"

Chris swallowed a huge bite of banana and ice cream, then answered, "Central America."

"You're kidding!" Katelyn and Jake looked at each other incredulously.

Chris shrugged, then spooned another bite of the gooey dessert into his mouth. "Nope. Why?"

Jake's voice intensified as he explained. "We've been talking about sending out a team to Central America for ages now, but the timing just hasn't been right. And we didn't really have a connection. Maybe you could give me some information while you're in town."

The two men dove into a lengthy conversation about Chris's work in Nicaragua. At several points along the way, Chris glanced at Adrianne to make sure she didn't feel left out. No, she seemed enthralled, as did Katelyn. Meanwhile, Lorelei, who at some point along the way had shifted out to the playground area with her friends, popped her head in the door every now and again to ask if they could stay longer.

When the adults wrapped up their discussion about water wells and remote villages, Jake looked over at Adrianne and smiled. "I like this friend of yours, Adrianne."

"He's a keeper," Katelyn said with a wink.

Chris noticed Adrianne's cheeks flush, and shot a glance over at the next table, hoping to distract everyone. "Looks like Lorelei's having fun."

"Oh, yes," Katelyn agreed. "She's very social, have you noticed?"

"I have." *Just like her mother.*

Katelyn added her thoughts on the matter. "Now that's one great kid. She has the sweetest spirit. She's the spitting image of her mother."

She is at that.

Jake chimed in with a gleam in his eye. "And I guess it goes without saying she's very talented."

"She is." Chris couldn't help but dive in. "And she sings just like her mother. You should have heard Adrianne back in college. She. . ." He caught himself just before giving too much away. Perhaps Adrianne didn't want her good friends knowing so much about her past.

"You never told us you sang, Adrianne." Katelyn turned to stare at her in surprise. "We would have signed you up for the worship team."

"Oh no." Adrianne threw her hands up in the air. "My singing days are behind me. Trust me."

"I wouldn't be so sure." Jake's smile seemed to light the room as he spoke. "It's a funny thing. Just about the time we say 'never again, Lord,' He opens a door."

"Or just the opposite," Katelyn suggested. "Sometimes when we're convinced that we know exactly what we're supposed to be doing, God sends us off on a detour in a completely different direction."

Whoa. A message for me, perhaps?

Chris leaned back in his chair and listened quietly as the pastor and his wife dove into an animated story of how they'd met on just such a detour. Every now and again, Adrianne would look Chris's way. When she did, her eyes seem to speak something. . . What was it? Hope? Longing?

Just about the time he thought he'd calmed his heart, Lorelei approached their table, stifling a yawn. Right away, Adrianne snapped to attention, glancing at her watch.

"Oh! It's nine thirty. We've got to get you home to bed."

"I'm not sleepy," Lorelei argued.

Adrianne stood, as if in response. "Sure you're not."

Chris stood alongside her, painfully aware of the fact that their time together was drawing to a close. In minutes, she would drop him off at the hotel and they would part ways.

For how long, he had no way of knowing.

❧

Adrianne gripped the steering wheel as they pulled away from the Dairy Queen. "Did you have a good time?" She glanced over at Chris, who nodded. She wondered at his silence over the past few minutes.

"I wish I didn't have to leave tomorrow." He turned to look at her, and even in the darkness, she noted the tremor in his voice. "I don't want to go."

"Do you have to leave?" Lorelei piped up from the back seat. "I want you to stay. Forever."

"Forever is a mighty long time." Adrianne tried to make light of the situation, but inside her heart was breaking. If Chris really boarded the plane the next morning, she didn't know what she would do.

Their conversation shifted a bit as they took turns talking about the day. Finally, when Adrianne was convinced her daughter had drifted off to sleep, she whispered a somber, "We need to talk," Chris's way.

"I know." His response, equally as soft, was accompanied by the touch of his hand brushing against her cheek.

She leaned against his hand and tried to still her heart. What in the world would she do without him, now that they'd found one another again?

And yet he had to go. He must return to his work on the mission field. Adrianne knew, beyond a shadow of a doubt, that she could never ask him to give it up, not after seeing the gleam in his eye as he talked to Pastor Jake about it. No, he must return to Nicaragua, and she must return to her life—as a single mother.

For a few minutes, she didn't speak. The lump in her throat wouldn't allow it. Finally, Chris broke the silence. "W–what are we going to do, Adrianne?"

She glanced back over her shoulder to make sure Lorelei was genuinely asleep before answering. "We'll. . .we'll work out a plan. You'll have to come back as often as you can. . . ."

"As often as I can?" The pain in his voice drove a stake through her heart, but she forged ahead.

"Yes. Whenever you're in the States, you'll have to come see us."

"And. . .that's it?"

She kept her focus on the road and willed herself not to cry. "I don't want you to miss out on anything. And you're welcome to be with us. . . ." Here her voice lowered. "With Lorelei. . .as often as you're able."

"And then?"

"I think she needs time to get to know you, and to get used to the idea that you're really her. . ." She mouthed the word *father*. Adrianne pushed back the lump in her throat. "And we both need time to pray and ask the Lord to show us what to do, right?"

"I'm going to do the right thing by both of you." He spoke firmly. "Financially, I mean. And in whatever other ways the Lord shows me. I need you to know that."

"You're a good man, Chris." She paused. "I—I know you're passionate about your work." Another pause gave her long enough to dab at her eyes and force down the lump in her throat. "We've just got to figure out how to balance the jungles of Nicaragua with historic Philadelphia, that's all."

"I don't know." He leaned his head back against the seat and sighed. "I know you love your work at the museum. It's obvious. You're amazing at what you do," he said, reaching out to touch her arm.

"So are you." She whispered the words, realizing all too well what she was saying. Whether they wanted to admit it or not, they were living in two very different worlds, going in two very different directions.

A painful silence filled the car as he released his gentle hold on her arm. The gesture seemed to speak volumes. As much as she hated to admit it, a separation of sorts had taken place. A wall had been erected, and it didn't appear to be coming down anytime soon.

With a sigh, she turned her attention back to the road.

sixteen

"Mom, where is Chris again?" Lorelei asked.

Adrianne looked up from underneath the bed where she'd been searching for her shoe. "I told you the last three times. . . ." A groan escaped her lips. "He had to go back to Virginia Beach. He's probably headed to the airport right now."

"Virginia Beach? How far is Virginia Beach?"

"Not close." Adrianne pushed back the lump in her throat and avoided her daughter's penetrating gaze. "Besides, I think he leaves for Nicaragua sometime later in the week. He was only here on a short furlough." She turned her attention back to looking for the missing pump.

"Furlough? What's that?"

"It's when a missionary comes home from the mission field for a short season. But he has to go back to Nicaragua." She spoke as much to convince herself as anything. "That's what missionaries do. They have to go wherever they feel the Lord is leading them."

Lorelei stepped closer, her voice trembling as she spoke. "But, Mom, I miss him. Can't the Lord lead him here?"

Well said, well said. "I suppose that could happen, but I wouldn't count on it."

"Isn't he coming back at all?"

Adrianne stuck her head under the bed once more in an attempt to reach the wayward shoe. Finally snagging it, she rose to her knees and stared at her persistent daughter. "I'm sure he'll be back sometime, but I couldn't say when."

"But, Mom,"—Lorelei sat on the edge of the bed, tears

coming to her eyes—"I wanted you to marry Chris. How can you marry him if he's in Nicaragua?"

Once again, Adrianne looked away as she spoke, focusing on the shoe, not the child. "What's your hurry to get me married off?" she asked finally.

Lorelei lifted her chin, defiant. "I want to have a dad. Someone to drive me to school every day. And come to my ballet recitals."

"I walk you to the bus stop every day. And you don't even take ballet."

"I would. If I had a dad."

Adrianne felt the sting of tears in her eyes, but quickly forced them away. *She only wants what every little girl wants.* She contemplated her next words as she slipped on her shoe. "Sometime soon we're going to have a long talk about all that."

"We are?" Lorelei's brow wrinkled, as she looked her way.

"Yes." *I think it's about time you knew the truth. But this isn't the time or the place.* Adrianne glanced at her watch. "Oh no, not again. You're going to miss the bus if we don't hurry up."

They donned their jackets and reached for Lorelei's schoolbooks, then raced out of the apartment. No sooner did they arrive at the corner than the school bus pulled up.

"Have a great day, baby." Adrianne kissed Lorelei on the cheek.

"I love you, Mom." Lorelei climbed aboard the bus, then looked back with a wave as it pulled away.

Adrianne caved the moment her daughter disappeared from sight. For once, she didn't even try to hold back the tears. Her heart felt completely broken. She longed to see Chris again, to tell him how much she loved him. Needed him. But how? With his heart in Nicaragua, and hers in Philadelphia, they seemed destined to remain apart forever.

The tears continued to flow as she made her way to the car and then on to the museum. All along the way, she thought about her situation. She examined it from every conceivable angle. Still, no matter how hard she tried, she couldn't find a workable solution.

&

Chris boarded the small commuter plane with a heavy heart. He glanced down at his e-ticket as he shuffled through the crowd of people.

Twenty-two E. Oh, great. A middle seat again.

Moments later he found himself seated between a rather large gentleman in the aisle seat and a young girl, probably six or seven, in the window seat.

Not that he had time or energy to focus on others at the moment. His thoughts kept gravitating to Adrianne and Lorelei. *What am I doing on this plane?* The thought rolled around and around in his brain. *Why in the world don't I just get off of here and tell her how I really feel?* "How do I really feel?"

"Excuse me?" The stewardess gave him a quizzical look as she passed by. "Aren't you feeling well, sir?"

"Oh, I. . ." He looked up and shrugged. "I'm fine."

She went on by, and the pilot's voice came on with their flight information. Chris scarcely heard a word. He spent the next several minutes, thinking through everything that had happened over the past few days. In less than a week, his entire life had changed. But how did he feel about all he had learned, really?

Hmm. With the plane now taxiing down the runway, he paused to think, really think, about his heart, his feelings. His love for Adrianne was undeniable. And yet, she hadn't been completely honest with him from the beginning, had she? On the other hand, she had tried to reach him on several occasions over the years. Surely she needed his forgiveness as much as they both needed the Lord's.

And what about Lorelei? Clearly, the youngster adored him. But then again, she didn't know the truth about their relationship either, did she? Would she still love him, once she realized he was her "absent" father—the one she'd done without all these years?

Chris leaned his head back against the seat and closed his eyes. A silent prayer went up—a please-show-me-what-to-do-Lord prayer. He prayed for Adrianne, for her provision, her peace of mind, for direction. He then shifted his attention to Lorelei, praying at length for her well-being, emotionally, spiritually, and physically.

Finally, Chris began to pray about the decision he now faced. *Lord, I know You have all of this figured out, but I feel like I'm being torn in two. Half of me wants to be in Nicaragua. Half of me wants to be in Philadelphia.*

Even as he prayed, the image of Lorelei's face flashed before him. He remembered, all too clearly, the look in her eyes as he spun her around the dance floor of the ballroom at the Ben. Was it just two nights ago? Seemed like an eternity. But the image, now fresh in his mind, suddenly reignited his desire to play the role of father.

Just as quickly, Chris saw the faces of all the children he had ministered to in the villages of Nicaragua. After years of mentoring countless boys and girls, he had become a spiritual father to many. How could he leave them now? And who would take his place, if he opted to leave?

With his mind twisted up in knots, Chris turned his thoughts back to prayer. He clamped his eyes shut and dove back into a silent debate with the Almighty.

A few seconds later, a gentle voice from his right roused him from his catatonic state.

"Are you scared?"

Chris looked over at the little girl in the window seat. Her wide blue eyes riveted on his.

"Excuse me?" he asked.

"Are you scared of flying?"

"Oh. No." He offered up a weak smile. "No, I'm not scared."

"You looked scared." She flashed a broad smile, then pointed out the window. "But see? We're already up in the air. There's nothing to be scared of."

"We are, aren't we?" He glanced out of the window and then turned his attention back to the little girl once again. Was she all by herself? Traveling alone at such a young age?

As if reading his mind, she chattered away, answering all of his questions before they were even voiced. Her name was Hannah. She was traveling to Norfolk to see her father for a few days. She and her mother lived in Perkasie, about an hour and a half north of Philly. She had never flown alone before, but needed to get used to it, now that her parents were divorced.

Whoa.

As she rambled on and on, Chris let his thoughts drift. *Lord, I don't want this to happen to Lorelei. I don't want her boarding planes alone, flying halfway across the world just to see a father she barely knows. I want her to know me. I want to know her.*

Just after the pilot's voice came on, informing the passengers of a rocky flight ahead, Chris closed his eyes once more in an attempt to sleep. As the plane began to tremor, Hannah grabbed his arm, rousing him from his near-slumber.

"Do you think there's a God?" she asked.

"What?"

"Do you think there's a God?" Hannah's voice grew more serious as she gazed out the window at the clouds.

"I do." The plane continued to vibrate and her grip on his arm intensified.

"Do you think He lives out there?" She let loose long enough to point out to the darkened clouds.

"Actually. . ." Chris smiled, as he pondered his response. "I think He lives in here." He pointed to his heart and Hannah looked over at him in curiosity.

"Huh?"

As the plane rocked and tipped, Chris took the opportunity to explain, in childlike terms, the full plan of salvation. Hannah's eyes widened as he told her about Jesus and His sacrifice on the cross. She smiled broadly when he explained that she could ask Him to live in her heart. And she even whispered a soft prayer to do just that—right there in the window seat.

As the bumpy ride settled down, the youngster turned back to look at the clouds once again. Before long, she drifted off to sleep. Chris closed his eyes and leaned back against the seat once more, finally ready to relax.

"Do you really believe all that stuff?"

This time the voice came from his left. Chris opened his eyes and gazed into the somber face of the man in the aisle seat.

"Excuse me?"

The portly fellow closed his magazine and stuffed it in the back of the seat in front of him. "All that stuff you were spouting. You believe that?"

Chris swallowed hard before answering, not wanting a confrontation, particularly in front of the sleeping child. Still, he needed to address the question at hand. "I do," he said finally.

"Then you're a fool." The man tilted his seat back and closed both his eyes and his mouth, as if that settled the whole thing.

An invitation to spar, perhaps?

"What do you mean?"

The fellow gave him a sideways glance, sort of an I'm-not-sure-you'd-really-get-it look. "I used to believe all that stuff about God," he explained. "About forgiveness. Before. . ." He shook his head, the already-deep wrinkles in his forehead deepening further still.

"Before what?"

The fellow looked over to make sure Hannah was asleep before responding. "Before my wife died of cancer."

Ah. Handle delicately, Chris.

He spent the next few minutes ministering to the man, speaking softly, and asking the Holy Spirit to guide every word. He deliberately chose not to slip into a preaching mode—even when the man, who introduced himself as Pete, got defensive. Chris simply did what he often found himself doing on the mission field; he met the man right where he was.

By the time the plane landed, Pete had opened up, sharing a few of his hurts, his pains. He confessed his anger with God, and his frustration with the doctors involved in his wife's care. He talked about his strained relationship with his grown children, how the whole family had grown apart since their mother's death.

Something interesting happened as the conversation drew to a close. Chris found himself sharing words of love, not as a missionary, but just as a friend. And the Spirit of the Lord rocked him to the core with an interesting new thought as he exited the plane behind his new friend.

"Don't you see, son? The mission field is everywhere— everywhere you happen to be. I can use you wherever you go, whether it's in the fields of Nicaragua or on an airplane. It's a ready heart I'm looking for. That's all."

Funny. Just knowing that suddenly put a lot of things in perspective.

seventeen

Adrianne stayed as busy as she could in the days following Chris's departure. The upcoming fundraiser dinner proved to be the perfect distraction. She and Dani worked together day in and day out, settling last-minute issues with the caterer and working alongside the party planner they'd hired to transform the lobby of the museum into a lovely banquet room.

Joey stayed close by, offering both humor and a helping hand. He proved to be a nice distraction, too, always giving her something to laugh about.

Still, in the quiet moments, when no one else was around, her heart ached for Chris. Many times during the day she would find herself wondering where he was, what he was doing. And why he hadn't called.

Frustrated, she forced her attention to the task at hand. Mr. Martinson was counting on her. The museumgoers were counting on her. She wouldn't let them down.

The following Friday night, Adrianne donned the same beautiful dress she'd worn to the rehearsal dinner and prepared to leave for the banquet. She found her nerves in quite a state—in part, because so much rode on tonight's event, and in part, because she hadn't heard from Chris in more than a week.

Maybe I'll never hear from him. Maybe he'll turn out to be a deadbeat dad, like so many others.

As she prepared to leave the house, her cell phone rang. She answered it with some degree of impatience.

"Ms. Russo?" The familiar voice greeted her. "James Kenner here."

Ah. "Mr. Kenner. Has something happened?"

"Oh no. Nothing like that. I was just wondering. . . ." His voice changed from businesslike to familiar in a flash. "I was just wondering if you might like a ride to the museum."

"Oh." She stumbled a bit through the rest. "I—I don't think that's necessary. See, I have to drop off my daughter at my mom's house, and I couldn't expect you to do that. It's not even on the way."

"I'd love to."

Now what do I do?

"There are some things I'd like to talk over before we get to the dinner—things having to do with the implementation of the grant money. Sorry to have to bore you with business, especially on a night like tonight, but this is important."

Sure it is.

"If you'll give me your address, I'll pick you and your daughter up in, what do you think, twenty minutes?"

"Hmm." Adrianne's mind raced. She grappled with many confusing thoughts, not the least of which was the idea that this guy could turn out to be anything but what he presented himself to be. "Tell you what," she said finally, "I'll meet you at the coffee shop on the corner near my apartment complex. That way you won't have to mess with the code for the security gate. Sound okay?"

"Sounds perfect."

She relayed the directions and he ended the call with a joyous, "See you soon, then."

As she snapped the cell phone shut, Adrianne slapped herself in the head. "Why in the world did I just do that?"

"Do what, Mom?" Lorelei entered the room with a portable video game in her hand.

Adrianne shook her head and sat on the sofa with her shoes in her hand. "That was a man I work with. He's picking us up."

"Why?"

Why, indeed? "It's a work thing," Adrianne explained. "He wants to talk to me about the museum. He's going to drive you over to Grandma's and then we'll go on from there."

"In his car?"

"Yes."

Lorelei shrugged. "Okay, Mom." She turned her attention back to the video game.

Twenty minutes later, mother and daughter entered the coffee shop. The whole place was alive with activity. People stood at the counter, ordering up every conceivable type of coffee. The place, which smelled delicious, calmed Adrianne's nerves at once.

She looked through the crowd until her gaze fell on James Kenner. "Ah. There he is," she said.

"He's handsome, Mom," Lorelei whispered.

Handsome didn't seem to be an adequate word. In his black tuxedo with his dark wavy hair carefully groomed, James Kenner looked like something from a magazine.

"Adrianne." He extended a hand as she approached, his amber eyes alight with joy. "You look amazing." He looked down at Lorelei and smiled. "And you must be. . ."

"Lorelei." The youngster stuck out her hand, and he took it for a firm handshake.

"Lorelei, it's great to meet you. I'm Mr. Kenner." He offered up a playful smile as he asked, "Are you a coffee drinker?" He gestured toward the crowd of people with countless cups of coffee. "Could I order something for you?"

She giggled. "No. I can't drink coffee. I'm just a kid." She looked up at her mom with a smile, then whispered, "But sometimes my mom lets me have just a little."

Adrianne felt compelled to explain. "Actually, I just give her a glass of warm milk with a teensy-tiny bit of coffee in it."

"It's yummy!" Lorelei added.

James laughed. "You two are funny. I like you." He flashed a dazzling smile in Lorelei's direction. "I'll call you Latte for short. Is that okay?"

She shrugged. "Okay."

James now looked at Adrianne. She felt his gaze sweep her from head to foot, and a flush warmed her cheeks as he asked, "Are we ready to go?"

"Sure." Adrianne draped her wrap over her shoulders. "Let's get this show on the road."

Lorelei chattered all the way to her grandparent's house, telling Mr. Kenner about her role in the church play, her video games, even her passion for cooking. Adrianne wondered if she might be wearing on the poor fellow's nerves, but he seemed to take the youngster's enthusiasm in stride.

"See you later, Latte!" he said as they dropped her off at the house.

"Later, gator!" she responded.

Adrianne glanced at her watch as they left her parents' house. "Yikes. We've got to get going. I'm going to be late."

"I won't let that happen." James chuckled. "No damsels in distress in this car."

They settled into an easy conversation, and Adrianne relaxed, in spite of everything. She took in the man to her left. He appeared to be genuinely nice. Clearly, he hadn't been as interested in talking business as she'd hoped, though he did managed to bring up the grant money and the banquet a couple of times.

As they drew near the museum, James glanced her way, and a shy look crossed his face. After a moment of silence, he finally stammered, "You. . .you look amazing, Adrianne." He offered an admiring gaze. "I really mean that."

"Thank you." She felt her cheeks warm.

"And I haven't had a chance to tell you this yet, but I'm so impressed with the way you've pulled together this evening's event. I hear you've been working round the clock."

"Yes." Thank goodness. *It's kept me sane for the past week since Chris*— No. She wouldn't think about him. Not tonight.

"It's going to be wonderful," James continued. "And a lot of my colleagues will be there. I've encouraged them to be *exceptionally* generous this year."

"Wow." Adrianne tried not to get too excited about his comments lest she be disappointed later. "We really just want people to give because they love the museum or admire our work there."

"There are a great many things to admire." James looked over at her with a penetrating gaze and she understood his meaning at once.

"I—I . . ."

"Promise me one thing, Adrianne." He took hold of her hand and gave it a squeeze. "When this is all over with, promise me you'll let me take you out for a celebration dinner. Say, one night next week?"

"Oh, I don't know—"

"Or the week after. Seriously, I won't take no for an answer. You've worked so hard. You deserve a night out to celebrate. And besides"—he feigned a back-to-business face—"we still have a lot to talk about."

Yes, but we're not talking business now, are we?

Adrianne leaned back against the seat and prayed her stomach would settle down before the evening's events got underway. They arrived at the museum in record time. The entire lobby had been transformed. Adrianne gasped as she saw it, then rushed to Dani's side. "It looks amazing in here."

"I used a lot of your ideas, so of course it looks amazing."

Adrianne looked up at the large swags of fabric and

twinkling lights, and then shifted her gaze to the many dining tables, each fully decked out with fine china and crystal. The whole place was absolutely magical—like something out of a. . .a fairy tale.

"Just pray this works," she whispered. "We need funds to come in."

"I've already prayed," Dani assured her. "Stay calm, Adrianne. Tonight is a night for relaxing. Celebrating." She chuckled. "Okay, and maybe a little arm wrestling with a few deep-pocketed patrons, too."

She nodded, then glanced to her right as her boss made his appearance.

"We rarely get to see you in a tux, Bob," she acknowledged.

"Yeah. I can't stand 'em, but my wife made me." He pulled at his bow tie with a grunt. "Said it'd be good for business."

"She was right."

He chuckled, then looked around the room. "Adrianne, the place looks great. Great. I've heard nothing but complimentary things from our guests."

"Really? I'm so glad."

Just then, James slipped in behind her, sliding an arm over her shoulders. "She's quite a girl, isn't she?" The words were meant for Mr. Martinson, but his eyes twinkled in Adrianne's direction.

"She is." Bob gave her a wink, then turned his attention to James. "Mr. Kenner"—he extended his hand—"we can never thank you enough for all the work you did on that grant. You've been a tremendous asset to the museum, and we're all very grateful."

"My pleasure. I've always loved this museum." James released his hold on Adrianne's shoulder to shake Bob's hand. "But never more than lately. There are a great many things here to draw my attention." He shifted his gaze, just for a moment, back to Adrianne.

Bob looked up with a fatherly glance, and Adrianne felt her cheeks flush.

"Well, I should head on over to chitchat with some of the others," he said. "I've got a little hobnobbing to do."

As he moved on to greet the other guests, Adrianne turned to face James. Just as she opened her mouth to tell him that he had embarrassed her, Joey joined them.

"Hey." He gave a little whistle as he saw Adrianne's dress. "You look amazing."

"Thank you." She gave a little twirl, but immediately wished she hadn't. The eyes of both men now locked firmly on her.

For a moment, anyway. After just a few embarrassing seconds, Dani cleared her throat. "Well, I. . .um. . .I'd better go check on the caterers."

Adrianne did her best to alleviate the awkwardness. She reached to give Joey's hand a little squeeze. "I know you had a lot to do with this. Thank you so much for helping set up the room."

"No problem. I'd do anything for y—the museum," he stammered. "You know that."

"Well, it turned out great, and I just want to give thanks where thanks are due."

Joey reached over to give her a warm hug, and for the first time since meeting him, Adrianne saw James Kenner's expression shift from genteel to perturbed.

What in the world?

Joey pulled back but never lost his focus. She looked at him with an uncomfortable smile, wishing she could just this once pull a Cinderella and run from the room.

Nope. Too awkward. She must stay put, no matter how difficult. As Adrianne stood there, with one man to her right and another to her left, she suddenly wished, for all the world, she could have the one in the middle, the one on the other side of the world.

Prince Charming.

❧

"Chris, my friend, I can't tell you how happy we are to have you back. We were at a loss without you."

Chris looked across the dinner table at fellow missionary David Liddell, and shrugged. "Looks like you did pretty well when I was away. I see a lot of progress."

David shook his head. "Things are never the same when you're on furlough. But I know you deserved the break." He flashed a warm smile. "And I do hope you had a good trip back to the States."

"I did." Chris's thoughts shifted at once to Adrianne. His trip had presented some interesting challenges but some unexpected blessings, as well.

"How was the wedding?"

"Oh, great. Stephen and Julie were wonderful hosts, and the ceremony was beautiful. I wish you could have seen the church. I'm not sure you would have believed it, especially after some of the buildings we've worked on here. It was amazing."

David let out a lingering sigh. "I know Stephen will be happy, married and living in the States, but I just keep thinking about him when he first came to Managua five years ago. I don't remember ever seeing such excitement in a young missionary's eyes."

"Right. I remember."

"We had some great years together."

"We did," Chris agreed, "but God has called him to a different season now."

"Right." David grew silent. Finally, he looked up with a smile. "Did you get some rest when you were in Philly?"

"Um. . .not really. No."

"Hmm. I was hoping you'd come back rested and refreshed. We've got a lot on our plates over the next few weeks. The church in Masaya is really struggling. I'm going to make a trip down there in a couple of days and hoped I could talk you into coming with me."

"Sure." Chris answered more out of rote than passion. For whatever reason, he couldn't quite seem to get back into the swing of things since his arrival in Managua a few days ago.

"I hear Pastor Alejandro is in need of some building supplies," David continued, "so we'll load up the truck before we go. Oh, and one more thing"—he glanced at his watch—"I've got to get over to the airport to pick up Brent in a few minutes. He's on the 8:15 flight."

"Brent?" *Who's Brent?*

"Brent Ferguson. He's from California, originally, but I understand he's done a lot of missions work in Guatemala and has a lot of experience with some of the more remote Spanish dialects. He's married to a nurse."

"Wow."

"He wants to join us for a couple of weeks to see what we're all about."

"I see." *Well, at least we won't have to train him. That's a relief.* "Where is he staying?"

David gave him a knowing smile.

"Oh no." Chris slapped himself in the head. "He's staying with me?"

David offered up a shrug. "It's either that or a hotel. There's too much construction going on over at my place. And I didn't have the heart to ask him to pay for a hotel room for two weeks."

"Two weeks?" Chris groaned.

"Yep. But don't worry, Chris. He's a nice guy, and he loves

the Lord. And he has a heart for this kind of work. I know you'll enjoy getting to know him."

"I'm sure you're right."

Chris wished he could garner up even half of David's excitement, but found his attention drawn to other things. He couldn't stop thinking about Adrianne and Lorelei. What were they doing right now, at this very moment? Were they eating dinner? Was Adrianne helping Lorelei with her homework?

Where are they?

And why am I here, so far away from them?

eighteen

Adrianne paced across her parents' living room, wearing a path in the carpet. For several minutes, she had struggled with whether or not to tell Adrianne about Chris. Her thoughts on the matter shifted back and forth, much like her emotions over the past week, since his departure.

She muttered her thoughts aloud, grateful the room was empty. "If I tell her that he's her father and he doesn't play that role in her life, she'll be even more hurt, more disappointed than ever."

Back and forth Adrianne walked, her thoughts rambling.

"On the other hand, if I don't tell her the truth about who he is, then I'm not being completely honest with her. And she's old enough now for me to be open and honest, even about something this difficult."

Adrianne paused to look out of the window, thinking she'd heard a car pull up in the driveway. *Just Dad starting the car. He's ready to go and I'm holding him up. And for what? I'm not making any progress, anyway.*

She continued on with her ponderings as she marched from one side of the room to the other. "I'm going to tell her. It's just a matter of time. I need to make sure I do this at exactly the right time and the way the Lord wants me to. I don't want to hurt her. That's the last thing I'd want to do."

"Mom, are you coming?" Lorelei entered the room, dressed in blue jeans and a matching jacket. Her eyes glistened with excitement, and her ponytail bobbed up and down as she clapped her hands in glee. "It's time to go."

126

"Mm-hmm."

"Grandma says you're lollygagging. What does that mean?"

"She's trying to say I'm taking too much time. But I'm coming now." *If my mom knew what was going through my mind, she would give me the time.*

"Grandpa says all the fish in the river will be gone if we don't leave soon."

"Okay, okay."

As Adrianne started toward the door her cell phone rang. Her heart flip-flopped as she reached to grab it from her purse. *Finally.* She had waited for Chris to call for days, and now. . .

She glanced at the number and groaned. James Kenner. Should she take it or let voicemail pick it up? If she didn't take it, he would probably be offended. She responded on the fourth and final ring with an all-too-cheery hello.

"Adrianne." His voice dripped with sweetness. "I'm so happy you're there. I was hoping I would catch you."

"Actually, we were just heading out," she explained. "My parents are taking us fishing this morning."

"Oh." The usual lilt in his voice all but disappeared. "Well, I understand. I had such an amazing time with you last night, and I was. . .well. . .just hoping we could spend the day together."

"I'm sorry." Adrianne glanced at her watch: 8:15. Her mother and father had already been waiting in the car a good five minutes.

"Wait, I have an idea!" James practically sprinted through the next few words. "I have a great little boat. The Pocket Yacht. I keep it at the Delaware River Yacht Club. What if I met you and your family there in, say, half an hour?"

"Oh, James, I don't know."

"Please let me do this, Adrianne." His tone softened a bit. "I want to meet your parents. And I know Latte would love the boat. They were made for each other. Besides"—he sounded remarkably coy, even a little embarrassed—"I really want to get to know you. Outside of our work environment, I mean."

"James, I—"

At that moment, Adrianne's dad entered the room with a frown on his face. He gestured to his watch, and then shrugged, as if to say, "What's taking so long?"

"James, my dad is right here. If you'll hold on a minute, I'll run this by him. I'll be right back."

She quickly relayed the information he had given her, praying her father wouldn't take the bait.

"A yacht?" Her father's eyes grew wide. "Are you kidding? Of course we'll go. I'll tell your mother." He bounded from the room, a smile as broad at the Atlantic on his face.

Good grief. Men and their boats.

Adrianne turned her attention back to the call, wishing with everything inside of her that she hadn't taken it in the first place. "James," she spoke with a sigh, "we'll meet you at the Yacht Club in thirty minutes."

At that very moment, another call came through. She didn't take the time to look at it, since James was still talking. "Do you know where it is?" he asked.

Sadly, yes.

The lilt in his voice continued on. "I could give you directions, if you like."

Another *beep* in her ear let Adrianne know the second caller was still trying to get through.

"No, that's okay. I know where it is."

Another *beep*.

"Wonderful." The happiness in his voice was genuine. "I'll see you then."

"Yes. See you soon." As she clicked off, Adrianne tried to

take the other call, but found the caller had already hung up. She glanced at the Caller ID. *Hmm.* "Restricted call?" What in the world did that mean?

Frustrated, she reached for her sweater and then sprinted toward the car.

ᨀ

Chris's heart thumped out of control as Adrianne's voice-mail kicked in. He listened intently to it, loving the lyrical sound of her voice. After the *beep*, he left a message, his nerves driving the words.

"Adrianne, this is Chris. I was hoping to reach you. I want. . . no, I need to talk to you. I miss you so much. I miss Lorelei so much. I wish I hadn't gotten on that—" Just as he tried to say the word *plane* a *beep* rang out and the message ended.

"No way." Should he call her back, try her home number?

What he would say when he found her was still unclear. Perhaps the Lord would give the right words in the right moment. One thing was for sure, he couldn't put off talking to her one moment longer. His heart wouldn't allow it.

Just as he reached in his wallet to search for her home number, Brent entered the room. "Are you ready?"

"Hmm?"

"David said we're supposed to be at the church in Masaya by late afternoon. I figured you'd be raring to go."

"Oh, I don't know." Chris clicked the phone off and placed it back on the stand. "To be honest, I'm completely unfocused. I've got a ton of other things on my mind today. I really don't know what good I'd be out on the field."

"I guess I could go in your place," Brent offered. "Or. . ."

Chris looked up, puzzled.

"Or, I could drive and you could talk. I've got pretty broad shoulders, and it looks like you just need someone to bounce things off of. Maybe God has sent me here for that very reason."

"God sent you all the way to Nicaragua to listen to me ramble on about my love life?" Chris chuckled. "Man, you've got a great sense of humor."

"Ah." Brent gave him a knowing smile. "This is about a woman?"

Chris nodded and Brent crossed his arms with a knowing look on his face. "Then I *know* the Lord has sent me here. My wife and I have only been married three years, but I could tell you just about anything you want to know about balancing marriage and missions work. So, let's get a move on. I'll do the driving, you do the talking."

"Okay. I guess." Chris reluctantly agreed, though he secretly wondered what in the world a total stranger might have to tell him about something so personal.

No sooner than they'd climbed into the truck to set out for Masaya, Brent shot a probing stare his way. "Okay, I'm waiting."

"Man, you get right to it, don't you?"

"Yeah. I figure you've got a captive audience, so why not go for it?" His expression softened a bit. "Seriously, Chris. You just tell me whatever you're comfortable sharing, nothing more."

I don't know how comfortable I am sharing anything with a total stranger.

Chris began, tentatively at first, then increasing in both courage and emotion. He told Brent every sordid detail of his relationship with Adrianne, all the way back to the beginning. He shared the part of losing touch and, more importantly, the part about finding her again.

And Lorelei. He shared, with a smile on his face, no less, the story of discovering the daughter he never knew existed. Brent didn't interrupt, but Chris could see the look of surprise on his face as he voiced his story. *Looks like maybe I've stumped*

*him after all. This isn't your run-of-the-mill missionary story,
after all.*

After hearing everything Chris had to say, Brent slowed
down and pulled the car off the road. Then he turned to give
Chris an inquisitive look.

"What is your heart telling you?"

Chris rubbed at his temples, unable to voice the words on
his heart. "I don't know," he whispered. "I just know that I
can't imagine living without them. Every time I think about
it. . ." A lump the size of the San Cristobal volcano grew in
his throat. "Every time I think of going one more day without
them, I feel sick inside. Everything feels wrong."

"But?"

"But the obvious. My work. I'm called to this organization.
I'm called to work with *these* children, here in Nicaragua."

Brent nodded, and drew in a deep breath. Then he looked
Chris. "I want to remind you of something," he said finally.
"Something I know you already know, but probably just need
to hear."

Chris looked up, not even trying to hide the moisture in his
eyes.

"We are all called to preach the gospel," Brent said. "All
believers. The Great Commission isn't just for people with
special degrees, or men and women who've applied to particular
missions organizations. 'Go into all the world' means just that.
And maybe, just maybe, the 'world' you're supposed to go into
is different than what you thought."

Chris felt his heart drop. "I—I can't believe God would call
me away from Central America. I love it so much. I love these
kids so much. I just wish I could. . ." He fought for words, but
none would come.

"Have your cake and eat it, too?"

He looked at his new friend with a sigh. "Yeah. That's it.

I want Adrianne and Lorelei, but I want this, too."

"So, why not do both?"

"Oh, I can't bring them here. It's out of the question."
He dove into a lengthy explanation, which Brent quickly
squelched.

"I'm not saying you should bring them here. I'm just asking
you to consider the possibility that your work here could
change somewhat to accommodate a new plan, a plan that
includes a wife and daughter."

"I don't know what you mean." Chris stared Brent down.

With a great deal of excitement, Brent began a detailed
explanation of just how he felt this whole thing could actually
work. Chris listened intently, especially when his new friend
asked him to open the Bible and turn to James, the first
chapter, verses five and six.

"Read it out loud," Brent encouraged him.

Chris turned the pages to the passage and glanced down at
the familiar words, understanding their significance in a new
way. " 'If any of you lacks wisdom,'" he read aloud, " 'let him ask
of God, who gives to all liberally and without reproach, and it
will be given to him.'" Chris glanced over at Brent with a smile.
"Sounds so easy."

"Keep reading."

" 'But let him ask in faith, with no doubting, for he who
doubts is like a wave of the sea driven and tossed by the
wind.'" With a sigh, Chris looked up. "That's what I've been
feeling like, a wave tossed around by the wind."

"That's why I love verse five so much," Brent said with a
smile. "God has a specific formula for stilling the waves of
doubt. Whenever I'm in a position where I don't know what
to do, which way to go, I ask the Lord to give me supernatural
wisdom. I know He will, because the verse says that God
gives generously to all without finding fault."

"Wow." Chris allowed those words to sink in. *"Without finding fault."*

"Do you think it's possible"—Brent gave him a pensive look—"that you've been afraid to ask God for the very thing you want the most because you feel in some way you don't deserve it?"

Man, this guy is good. "Well, I—"

"Because we serve a God who longs to give us the desires of our heart."

"As long as they're not selfish desires," Chris threw in.

Brent shook his head. "I don't believe for a moment your desires are selfish. You long to have a family, and you long to minister. Those are two bona-fide desires. And they're godly desires, too." He dove into a lengthy dissertation about God's views on family and ministry, sharing more of his thoughts on Chris's specific situation. When he finished, Chris suddenly felt the issue settled in his spirit.

"I know you're right. God has forgiven me for the things of the past, and He loves me. And I know He has all of this figured out."

"Then let's pray for wisdom." Brent prayed aloud as they drove, asking the Lord to reveal His perfect will. Afterward, the two men once again began to talk about the particulars of combining family and ministry. Before long, a full-fledged plan emerged, one clearly sent from On High.

Within ten minutes, Chris couldn't stop the smile from creeping across this face. Within twenty minutes, he drummed his fingertips on the door of the vehicle, and bounced ideas off of his new friend. Within thirty minutes, he was ready to catch the next flight to Philadelphia.

nineteen

"Pastor Jake, could I talk to you and Katelyn for a minute after service today?" Adrianne hoped he didn't notice the trembling in her hands as she spoke.

"Sure, Adrianne." Jake flashed a smile. "Want to meet in my office? You know how crazy it gets in the sanctuary after service. Everyone hangs around for ages."

"Sure. That'd be great."

He turned toward the podium and took a few steps, then turned back again with a concerned look on his face. "Is everything okay?"

She nodded slowly, then shrugged. "I just need someone to talk to," she said. "And I know you two will give me great advice."

"Okay. We'll see you there."

Adrianne somehow made it through Jake's sermon, although his "Love Conquers All" theme only added to her dilemma.

So many thoughts rolled around in her head. She reflected on them all—the look on Chris's face the night she'd told him about Lorelei, the pain in her heart when he'd left days later, and the confusion over James's unwelcome attentions, both at the fundraiser dinner and aboard his yacht yesterday.

"Lord, I need your wisdom. I'm so confused, and yet. . ."

In her heart, she knew the one thing that made sense in the middle of all of this. Sitting in church last week, with Chris's hand in her own, watching their daughter onstage, singing her heart out. . .

Now, *that* felt right.

The service came to a close, and Adrianne sent Lorelei off with her parents so that she could meet with Jake and Katelyn. She beat them into his office but was too nervous to sit. He finally arrived, his wife at his side. Jake settled down in the chair behind his desk, and Katelyn and Adrianne sat in the wing-backed chairs across from him.

"All I have to do is look at your face to see that something is up," Katelyn said. "So what's on your heart, Adrianne?"

Adrianne drew in a deep breath before starting. She wanted to do the best possible job, presenting this story, not deliberately swaying her friends one way or the other.

"It's kind of a long story," she said. "And it starts eight years ago."

She told them, no words minced, about her relationship with Chris back in college. Katelyn eyes grew large, but she didn't say anything, not at first, anyway. Adrianne told them both about the sin she and Chris had entered into, and how she had left the school to return to Philadelphia.

"I've struggled with feelings of guilt for years," she acknowledged, "but I know the Lord has forgiven me. He's done an amazing work in my life."

"And in Lorelei's life, too," Jake added. "She's pretty special."

"Yes. She's an angel, that girl." Katelyn offered a reassuring nod.

"I know. But thank you for saying it. I often wonder what I ever did to deserve her." Adrianne dove back into her story, telling her friends about the many times she had tried to reach Chris. When she got to the part of the story where he had "coincidentally" shown up at the museum, Katelyn's eyes widened again.

"Oh, my. Looks like God set that one up."

"Yes. That's what my dad said, too." Adrianne then shared all that had transpired since Chris's arrival in Philadelphia, how she had told him about Lorelei, and how he had responded. She closed out the story with tears in her eyes as she shared the part where he'd left town, heading back to Nicaragua. "I don't know when I'll see him again," she whispered.

Katelyn looked into her eyes, love pouring forth as she spoke. "Adrianne, I want to tell you something. Last week, when we met Chris for the first time, I just had this, this *sense* that he was more than a friend. I'm not sure how I knew, but I did."

"Really?" Adrianne shook her head, amazed.

"There was something about the way he looked at you." Katelyn's lips curled up in a smile. "And, to be honest, your face was lit with joy every time you looked at him, too."

"W—was it? I didn't mean to. . ."

"No," Katelyn said, "this wasn't something you did consciously. This was a genuine caring look, like a wife would give her husband."

Adrianne felt her cheeks flush, but resisted saying anything.

"The two of you are very natural together," Jake agreed. "I definitely saw the friendship side of things, but wondered if there might be more."

"But what can we do?" Adrianne asked. "I mean, really? Is there a solution? We can't take Lorelei to the mission field."

"You already have." Jake looked intently into her eyes.

"What?"

"Every time we do an outreach, every time we bring inner-city kids into the church to see a play, every Christmas when we take gifts to children in the projects, she's on the mission field."

"But you know what I mean," Adrianne implored. "Nicaragua?"

Jake shook his head. "I don't think you'll be taking Lorelei to Nicaragua, at least not for good. But I do think she will see much of the world, once you and Chris are married. So will you, in fact."

"W–what?"

Jake smiled. "Look. Katelyn and I have been talking about this for days, ever since we met Chris. We really liked what we saw in him. And I think he'd be a great addition to our staff here. We could stand to have a missions pastor, especially one who's acquainted with Central America. And from everything he shared last week, I think he would do well, taking charge of all of our local inner-city missions projects, too."

"Are you serious? You had already planned to contact him?"

Katelyn nodded. "We were going to run this idea by you today, in fact. He could work here much of the time—in Philadelphia—and take teams to Central America three or four times a year."

Adrianne shook her head. "I—I don't know. His heart is in Nicaragua. He loves the children there. He could never leave them."

Now Jake shook his head. "I think you're wrong about that. A man with a true heart after God puts the Lord first, his family second"—he glanced at Katelyn—"and his ministry third. I honestly believe that Chris will come to the same conclusion, especially once he's had some time to think about it."

"But how could I expect that of him? He's not my husband. He's just—"

"The man you love," Katelyn whispered. "And the man who loves you. I have no doubt about that, especially now that you've shared your story. I can see the three of you—you, Chris, and Lorelei—ministering together all over the place."

"But how in the world could we minister with our background?" Adriane hung her head in shame. "People would never accept us. W–we messed up so many things."

"Haven't we all?" Jake stood, and began to pace the room. "I mean, no one is immune from a sinful past. No one. 'For all have sinned and fall short of the glory of God.' That's what the scripture says."

She nodded. "Right."

"I'll bet you didn't know that I was away from God while I was in my teens."

"What?"

"Yes. I was on drugs for three years. In fact, Katelyn wouldn't date me during that time—and rightfully so. She knew we were unequally yoked."

Adrianne looked over, amazed as Katelyn nodded. "I steered clear of him, to be honest. And it was hard. I loved him, even then. Prayed for him every day."

"The Lord got a hold of me when I was nineteen," Jake added. "I got cleaned up. Sobered up. And, man"—a look of joy filled his eyes—"I still remember the day I felt the Spirit of the Lord leading me to go into the ministry." He looked at Katelyn with a smile. "Do you remember that?"

"I do." She looked at Adrianne. "At first, I doubted he was really genuine about laying down the drugs and following the Lord, but thankfully I was wrong."

"Thank God," Adrianne whispered.

"Don't you see?" Jake reached over and put a hand on her shoulder. "That's why I feel so at home in this part of the city. That's why I want so desperately to reach out to those kids on the streets. I can relate to them, especially the ones who are struggling. And I'd be willing to bet Chris, once he really hears from God on the matter, will be the same. It might take some time for the two of you to see yourselves as useable, but don't wait forever. You said it yourself, Adrianne. God has washed away all of your sins. Right?"

"Right."

"And you love this man, right?" Katelyn asked.

"R–right," she whispered.

"Then prepare yourself," Katelyn said with a wink. "Because I have a feeling the Lord has already set the wheels in motion. Just pray, Adrianne. And we'll pray with you."

Jake and Katelyn took the time, right then and there, to pray. With great passion in his voice, Jake prayed that Chris would hear the voice of the Lord as never before. Katelyn prayed that Adrianne would have the faith, and the courage, to be still and allow God to be God.

And Adrianne prayed, too—that God would give her the right words to say to Lorelei, for the time was drawing near.

❧

"Are you ready, Chris?"

"Hmm?" Chris turned to face Brent, his heart beating wildly.

"You've been holding that phone for nearly fifteen minutes. Are you going to call her, or what?"

"Oh, I. . ." He stared down at the phone.

"Listen." Brent approached him and took the phone from his hand. "Let's talk this through. What are you going to say when you reach her?"

"I. . .uh. . ."

"Not great with words, eh?" Brent grinned. "Never fear. I'm here to help. Let me make a suggestion."

"Okay."

"Tell her that you are miserable."

"I am."

"You are. And tell her that God has been speaking to you through your friends."

"Good grief. Can't I just say that He's been speaking?"

"Whatever. Anyway, tell her that you can't live another day without her."

"Sounds like you've been working on this speech."

"I've used it before"—he flashed a grin—"with my wife. Before she was my wife, I mean."

"Ah."

"It's a good speech."

"And the part about the missions work?" Chris looked up for reassurance.

"Just what we talked about the other day. No more, and no less."

"Okay." He clutched the phone, then began to punch in her number. "I can do this. I can."

When Adrianne picked up after only two rings, it startled him so much that he almost dropped the phone. "H–hello? Adrianne?"

"Chris, is that you?" The joy in her voice spoke volumes. "I can hardly hear you."

"We must have a bad connection. But Adrianne, I have something to tell you. I haven't slept for nights, and I won't sleep tonight, either. Unless I tell you."

"Tell me? Tell me what?"

"I—I. . ." He looked up to find Brent nodding in encouragement. Chris stood and began to pace the room. "I have loved you from the day I met you. The first time I saw you walking across the campus, you were wearing a white blouse and a pair of jeans. Your hair was pulled back, but the wind was still blowing little bits of it in your face. I was with my buddies. I pointed across the parking lot and said, 'That's the girl I'm going to marry.'"

"I—I never knew that." The tremor in her voice gave him the courage to continue.

"It's true. And you will never know how scared I was to ask you out on that first date. Do you remember? We went out for pizza. I could hardly eat a bite."

"I remember."

"I remember so many things." His words began to speed up. "Like how much I loved hearing you sing on the worship team. How beautiful you looked whenever you lost your temper."

"Hey now. . ."

"How comfortable you were in my arms. And how amazed I was that someone like you would look twice at a lowly guy like me—a kid hoping to one day be a missionary."

"I was so proud of you, Chris," she whispered. "I still am."

His heart sailed at the words. "Thank you." After a brief pause, to offer up a silent prayer, he forged ahead. "I want to tell you something else, too—something that's easier to say now that I've had time to think. I am so proud of you for raising Lorelei the way you have. She's your clone, the spitting image of her mother."

"And her father."

"When I look at her"—Chris's eyes filled right away—"I see all of the possibilities for what we can be. Together."

"Oh, Chris—"

"Adrianne, I have to tell you something." His pacing stopped and the sweating began. "I have messed up so many things in my life, but I don't want to blow one more thing. I love you. I've loved you every minute of every day for over a decade. And I'm going to do the right thing. I'm going to—"

Just as he reached the pinnacle of his speech, the phone went dead in his hand. Chris looked at it in disbelief. "You've got to be kidding me," he muttered. He tried—panic leading the way—to dial the number again, only to find all circuits were busy. "No way!" He turned to face Brent, a shockwave running through him. "What in the world do I do?"

"Well, I guess there's really only one thing *to* do." Brent faced him head-on. "I guess you'll just have to tell her in person."

twenty

Adrianne hardly slept a wink on Sunday night. Instead, she tossed and turned, replaying Chris's words in her mind. *"I told my buddies, 'That's the girl I'm going to marry.'*

" *'The girl I'm going to marry.'* "

Her lips curled up in a smile. How she longed to know more. Did he still feel that way now? If so, would he act on those words? Why, oh why, had the phone call ended so abruptly? Would she never know?

A plan, of sorts, rolled through her brain at about three in the morning. At four, she arose from the bed and signed on to the Internet. As she clicked the Web address for airplane flights, her heart raced. "I must be crazy. I can't go to Nicaragua, can I?"

She stumbled around the site, trying to find a direct flight from Philadelphia to Managua. Nothing. She tried again, this time finding a flight with a brief layover in Atlanta.

"One thousand two hundred ninety-eight dollars? No way."

She continued on in her search, growing more frustrated by the moment.

"Slow down."

Adrianne heard the Lord's voice so clearly, it almost scared her. She leaned her head down onto the keyboard and wept. "Lord, I don't feel like slowing down. I want to see him. I want to. . . ," she stammered over the words. "I want to marry this man, spend the rest of my life with him. We've lost eight years already, eight years we could have been a family. I don't want to lose one minute more."

"Trust Me with all your heart. Don't lean on your own understanding."

"But, Lord. . ."

She took a few slow, deep breaths and attempted to calm down. After drying her eyes, the temptation to return to the Internet resurfaced. She resisted and shut down the machine altogether.

After pacing the living room for nearly half an hour, she finally wore herself out. With her eyelids now heavy, she headed back to the bedroom, where she, thankfully, dozed off. A couple of hours later, the alarm went off. She reached over to slap it, noticing the headache at once. After swallowing down a couple of aspirins, she leaned back against the pillows, hoping to catch a few more z's before waking Lorelei. She awoke to the sound of her daughter's shrill voice.

"Mom, I missed the bus!"

"W–what?" Adrianne sat up, shocked. She looked at the clock: 8:45. "No way. It was just six. Wasn't it?"

Lorelei pounced on the bed. "Do I have to go to school today? I'm already late anyway. Can't I just stay home?" She ping-ponged up and down on the bed, eyes blazing with excitement.

"You have to go to school," Adrianne admonished. "Regardless of the time. I'll write a note. Everything will be okay."

With a pout, her precocious daughter headed off to dress for school. Adrianne raced like a maniac around the room, trying to decide what to wear. Her navy suit was at the cleaners. Maybe the black slacks and brown sweater? "Hmm." She looked through her closet, finally settling on a tailored ivory jacket and slacks, with a sky blue blouse.

"Hurry, Lorelei!" she hollered as she dressed. "We're late!"

"I'm hurrying!" The youngster's voice rang out from down the hallway.

Moments later, Lorelei appeared at the bedroom door, dressed in a mismatched purple T-shirt and fluorescent orange pants. Her tennis shoes were a shocking pink, which really made the whole ensemble look more like a costume than school clothes.

"Oh: no." Adrianne shook her head. "You can't wear that."

"Why not?" Lorelei looked in the mirror. "I like these colors."

"You can't, because. . . Oh, never mind." Adrianne looked around the room, frustration mounting. "Can you help me find my shoes? I can never seem to find them when I need them."

"The ones you left in the living room last night?"

Adrianne sighed. "Yeah. Probably. Would you run and fetch them for me?"

As Lorelei sprinted down the hallway, Adrianne turned her attention to her makeup. She looked into the bathroom mirror, horrified at her swollen eyelids. "Oh no. Please, no." She pulled out the stick of concealer and ran a line of it under each eye. As she rubbed it in, she thought about her middle-of-the-night escapades. What would Lorelei say if she knew her mother had spent half the night thinking about flying off to Central America? What would her parents say? Would everyone think she had lost her mind?

"I found your shoes, Mom." Lorelei appeared with the familiar pumps in hand. She looked up, a curious look crossing her face. "You were crying, weren't you?"

"What?" Adrianne continued applying her foundation. "What makes you say that?"

"Your eyes are all puffy." Lorelei pointed at the reflection in the mirror. "I can always tell."

"Good grief." Adrianne smeared on some lipstick, then reached for her blush brush. "I didn't get much sleep last night. I tossed and turned."

"Why did you get on the computer?"

Good grief, again. Can't a woman have any privacy at all? "I, um. . ."

Lorelei crossed her arms and watched intently as Adrianne applied eye shadow to her swollen eyes. "You're keeping secrets."

"No, I'm not." *It's not like I actually bought a ticket. It's not like I'm going anywhere.*

"How come you couldn't sleep?" Lorelei leaned her elbows on the bathroom counter with an inquisitive look on her face. "Are you sick?"

Lovesick, maybe. "No, not really sick. I'm just—"

"You miss him, don't you, Mom."

"What? Miss who?"

"You know who. Prince Charming. Chris."

"I don't know why you keep saying that," Adrianne said. "And in order to make your little story work, I'd have to change my name to Cinderella."

"Ooh, Cinderella!" Lorelei agreed with a smile. "She's my favorite."

Mine, too. "Well, if I have to play the role of Cinderella, I'll have to dress in rags and sleep in the ash heap."

"Only until he rescues you," Lorelei said with a giggle. "That's the best part."

"And what makes you think I need to be rescued? I'm doing a pretty good job, don't you think? I put a roof over our heads, and the bills are paid."

"That's not everything."

Good grief. She really does sound like the mother, doesn't she?

Adrianne opted to change gears. "What makes you think it wasn't James Kenner I was thinking about?" She crossed her arms and gave her daughter an inquisitive stare.

"Oh, come on, Mom. Puh-leeze!"

"I thought you liked him."

Lorelei shrugged. "He's okay. He's handsome, but—"

"What?"

Lorelei wrinkled her nose. "He doesn't have your shoe size."

"Excuse me?"

"You know. He's not Prince Charming. He won't have a shoe that fits."

"Lorelei, you've been watching too many movies. And reading far too many fairy tales."

Her daughter shrugged. "You told me if I would read more it would make me smarter. And besides, I want you to get married some day. I want to have a dad."

Adrianne groaned. "Honey, we've had this discussion before. And I really don't have time right now. . . ."

Even as she spoke the words, reality, like a bolt of lightning, hit.

Slow down.

That's what the Lord had said. Slow down and. . .

Oh Father. Are You asking me to talk to her? Now? I don't have time. I don't have. . .

A thousand excuses ran through her mind. But less than a minute later, the truth won out. *Yes, Lord. I'll do it. And I'll do it now.*

She drew in a long, deep breath and turned to face her daughter. "You know what?" she said. "I think maybe, just maybe, it's okay to take our time. There's something I need to talk to you about."

"Cool!" Lorelei raced to the bed and sprang up on it, motioning for Adrianne to do the same.

With slow, deliberate steps, she made her way to where her daughter sat. Then, with her heart in her throat, she began.

"I know you've always wondered about your daddy," she started.

Lorelei nodded. "You said you would tell me someday."

"That's right." She swallowed hard. "And today is that day."

Lorelei's eyes grew large. "You're going to tell me about my dad?" She grabbed Adrianne's hand and squeezed it. "Tell me, Mom. I'm big enough. You can tell me."

"I know you're a big girl, and that's a good thing, because what I have to tell you is only for big-girl ears."

Lorelei pulled her knees up to her chest and sat in silent anticipation. Adrianne pushed back the tears and told her the very thing she had put off for years.

"Your father is a wonderful man," she said with a smile. "A man who looks a lot like you. He has your sense of humor." She reached to tuck a stray hair behind Lorelei's ear. "And he has a good heart like you do."

"Really?" Lorelei sighed. "But will I ever get to meet him?"

Adrianne closed her eyes and whispered a silent prayer before saying the words: "You already have."

Her daughter looked directly into her eyes, clearly confused.

"You met him that night at Grandma and Grandpa's house, and you met him again at the wedding the next day."

"Oh, Mom!" Lorelei reached to grab her hand. "Chris is—"

Adrianne nodded, the lump in her throat now the size of an apple.

"My daddy? He's my daddy?"

"Y–yes. He is. It's a long, long story, and one day I'll tell you more. But Christopher Bradley is your daddy. H–he didn't know about you."

"He didn't?" Another look of confusion registered. "Why not?"

"That's a long story, too. But from the minute he found out he had a daughter—from the minute he laid eyes on you—he loved you. He still loves you."

Lorelei's eyes misted over, and within seconds tears began. She leaned her forehead into her knees and sobbed openly. Adrianne slipped an arm around her shoulders and drew her close.

"But he's in another place now." Lorelei looked up, her damp cheeks now shining pink. "Doesn't he want to be here? With me? With us?"

Answer carefully, Adrianne.

"I know he wants to be with you, with both of us."

"He does?"

Adrianne nodded. "I know, because he called me from Nicaragua to tell me how much he misses us."

Lorelei leaned her head against Adrianne's arm. "Mom?"

"Yes?"

"Do you love him? Do you love Chr—my daddy?"

Adrianne smiled, and a warmth like she had never known flooded over her. "Oh, honey, I do. I love him so much. I've loved him for many, many years."

"Is that why you kept his picture in the drawer?"

A slight chuckle slipped out as she contemplated her answer. "Yes. I suppose so."

After a deep sigh, Lorelei looked up with a childlike grin. "I'm so happy, Mom. I am. Thank you for telling me."

Over the next half hour, Adrianne answered many of her daughter's questions. "No, Nicaragua isn't close." "Yes, your grandma and grandpa know." "No, we can't go see your daddy today." She smiled as she answered the last one. "Yes, I hope one day we will both change our last names to Bradley."

As they wrapped up their quiet conversation, Adrianne looked once again at the clock. "It's nearly ten," she said.

"Do I still have to go to—"

"Yes, you still have to go to school."

Lorelei sprang from the bed, her electric outfit catching a

shimmer from the morning sunlight at the window. "But I'm too excited."

Me, too. "I know. But we have to keep doing all of the usual stuff."

"Till when?" Lorelei asked.

"Till the Lord gives me clear directions," Adrianne said with a grin.

With a pout, Lorelei asked, "When will that be?"

"I haven't got a clue," Adrianne responded. "But I'll promise you this—when He tells me what to do, you will be the very first to know."

❧

Chris sat quietly among the mob of people in Atlanta's busy airport. Every few seconds he glanced down at his watch. Forty minutes till his flight. Thirty-five. Thirty.

A voice announced over the loudspeaker that passengers could begin boarding momentarily. As he stood to get in line, he toyed with the notion of calling Adrianne.

Nope. Don't call. Just surprise her.

Somehow, the idea of popping in on her just felt right. And the idea of asking her to be his forever felt even *more* right.

twenty-one

Chris's plane landed at the Philadelphia International Airport at exactly two fifteen in the afternoon. He raced to get his suitcase from baggage claim, then rented a car. All the while, he rehearsed the speech in his head, what he would say when he saw Adrianne. Within minutes he was on the turnpike, headed for the historic district. At three o'clock, he pulled into the Franklin Institute parking garage.

Before getting out of the car, he offered up a rushed but determined prayer. *Father, I put this into Your hands. Not my will, but Yours be done.*

As he made his way into the museum, Chris did everything in his power to squelch the knot in his stomach. It refused to budge. So did the tightness in his chest. No, he wouldn't be the same again until he held the woman he loved in his arms once more. Then all would be right with the world.

He found the museum more crowded than before. Several school groups milled about, hundreds of youngsters with name tags and frustrated teachers calling out to keep them in line.

"Excuse me." He edged past a little girl with red hair and freckles. She turned to give him an inquisitive stare. "Sorry," he added.

A boy with dark brown eyes glanced his way with wondering eyes. "Are you lost?" he asked.

"No," Chris responded. *In fact, I don't know when I've ever felt more found than right now, in this very moment.*

With excitement mounting, he worked his way through the

mob and went to the front desk, where he was met by a young woman with a clipboard in her hand. He glanced down at her nametag: DANI.

"Hi." He tried to steady his voice. "I–I'm looking for Adrianne Russo."

"Ooh." Dani's eyes grew wide. "You don't say."

"I do say."

"Well"—her lips curled up in a smile—"your name wouldn't happen to be Christopher Bradley, would it?"

He nodded, unable to speak. The joy at knowing Adrianne had told a coworker about him proved almost more than his nerves could take.

"I had a feeling," Dani said, her smile widening. "What a great day this is turning out to be."

Chris gave her an imploring look. "Can you take me to her?"

"She's working on a new display in the back of the museum," Dani explained. "It's off limits to visitors, but I'll take you there myself."

"Are you sure it's okay?"

"For you?" she said. "It's more than okay. To be honest, I can't wait to see the look on Adrianne's face."

"Um. . .me neither."

He tagged along on Dani's heels, winding in and out through the crowd of tourists. At one point, he almost lost sight of her, she was moving so quickly. They went through the Wright Brothers display and back into an area marked UNDER CONSTRUCTION, where Dani used her key to open a door.

They pressed through that door, and then turned right, where she opened another narrower one. Chris looked around, amazed to find himself inside a large display window. Adrianne stood with her back to him, working diligently to dress a mannequin in a Revolutionary War costume. He wanted to race toward her, but resisted the urge.

Dani put a finger to her lips and backed away. As she eased her way out of the door, she gave him a thumbs-up signal. Chris swallowed hard, and then prayed for courage to do the thing he had come to do.

"Adrianne." As the word leaped across his lips, it sounded like music to his ears.

She turned, with one hand on her heart and the other over her mouth. "C–Chris?"

For a second, neither moved. But then everything seemed to advance at warp speed. They met in the middle of the display case, where he swept her at once into his arms and began to plant soft kisses on her cheek. Her arms reached out to encircle his neck and their lips met in a kiss so familiar, it tilted him backward in time eight years.

How have I lived this long without her?

They lingered a moment in each other's arms before Adrianne looked up at him with a shy smile. "I—I knew you would come. I knew it."

"I had to. I thought I'd die if I didn't."

"I understand. You have no idea."

He smiled. "Oh, I think I do."

She brushed a soft kiss across his lips and then leaned her head against his. He reached with his fingertips to touch her cheekbone, tracing a familiar line of freckles. Finally, he pulled back to gaze into her eyes.

"I need to tell you something." When she nodded, he continued. "I didn't get to finish this on the phone, so I'm going to finish now."

"O–okay."

"I told you then that I'd loved you since the day I met you. But I didn't get to tell you the rest—that I'm not complete without you. I'm only. . ." He fumbled to get the words out.

"Half of what I should be. Half of what God created me to be. I thought my work would fill the emptiness inside of me, and to some extent it did. But I know now that I could never be truly whole without you."

"Oh, Chris"—she reached to grab his hands—"I've felt that way for eight years. It's been awful without you. I haven't been myself. I've been—"

"Lost." They spoke the word together.

"For awhile, I was lost in confusion," she acknowledged. "And then the grief took over. But the worst season of all was the one where I couldn't forgive myself. I lived for years like that. I—I didn't think I could ever shake it."

"I understand, trust me." He gazed into her eyes, wondering what in the world he had ever done to deserve her. "W–what do you think now? About the forgiveness issue, I mean."

"Ah." A lone tear trickled down her cheek. "These past few weeks God has shown me over and over again that He forgave me all those years ago—when I first asked—not just for the sexual sin, but for not trying harder to reach you. I should have done more."

Chris shook his head and kissed the back of her hand.

"His forgiveness I could accept," she continued. "Finally, anyway. *Mine* was harder, because I felt like I somehow had to earn it by being good. And I could never be good enough to please myself. Does that make sense?"

"You *are* good, Adrianne," Chris emphasized. "But it's not your goodness, or lack thereof, that matters. When God looks down at you—and me—He sees two people who are washed in the blood of His Son, forgiven of the past. If He can see us that way, well..."

"I know." She sighed, and then gazed up at him once more, love pouring from her eyes. "We've wasted so much time. So much."

"I'm not wasting a minute more." He reached into his pocket to pull out the tiny box. It held the same ring he had purchased—and intended to slip on her finger—ages ago in Virginia Beach.

As Chris dropped to one knee, his foot caught the edge of the curtain that had, until now, anyway, shielded the unfinished window display from the crowd on the other side. He didn't care. This had to be done, tourists or not.

"W–what are you doing?" Adrianne stared down at him in amazement.

"Exactly what I came to do. Exactly what I should have done when we were in college." With the ring box firmly gripped in his hand, he gazed up into her eyes. Pressing down the lump in his throat, he spoke: "Adrianne, I love you more than I ever knew it was possible to love another human being."

"I love you, too," she whispered in response.

Onlookers gathered on the other side of the window, but Chris tried to stay focused. "I've made a lot of mistakes. I know I don't deserve you. But I would be so honored—so honored—if you would. . ." He looked up, encouraged by the love pouring from her eyes. "Will you marry me, Adrianne?" The tears started at once and he reached to kiss her hand.

She knelt beside him and nodded, her eyes spilling over. "Yes." She whispered the word, then added, "Oh yes. I will." Her face lit into a broad smile as he pulled the ring from the box and slipped it onto her finger. She stared down at it, then whispered, "It's beautiful." She stared at it a moment longer before looking up at him, amazed. "I–I've seen this before somewhere."

"It was the summer before our senior year," he reminded her. "We were in the mall in Virginia Beach. Remember?"

Recognition registered in her eyes. "Everson's Jewelry."

He nodded. "You pointed to it and told me it was the

prettiest thing you'd ever seen."

"I remember. But, a—are you saying. . ."

"Yes." He nodded and she shook her head, clearly confused. "I went back that same afternoon and put it on layaway. Paid on it for weeks."

"I don't believe it," she whispered.

"I paid it off on a Tuesday," he said. "But I wanted to wait till Friday night to give it to you. It burned a hole in my pocket for days," he explained. "But then—"

"I left."

After he nodded, she gripped his hand and gazed intently into his eyes. "I've made so many mistakes, Chris. But this isn't one of them. This is the best thing that has ever happened to me."

Chris's heart began to sing. Adrianne, his Adrianne, now wore his ring. She would soon be his. And they, together, would raise their daughter. "W—when can we tell Lorelei?"

"Today. Right now, if you like."

There, with more than a dozen people looking on, they sealed the deal with a passionate kiss. Through the glass, Chris could hear the roar of the crowd as the applause began. Now, somewhat flustered, he looked out to discover the group outside had grown immensely.

"Um. . .Adrianne?"

"Yes?" She gazed into his eyes. He pointed through the glass. She looked out and offered up a little shrug. "Oh well. They paid the admission price. Why not?" She leaned forward and gave him one last playful kiss, then, together, they turned and waved to the crowd.

❧

Adrianne danced a jig on the inside as she and Chris left the Revolutionary War display. *He's here! He came for me. And I'm. . . engaged!*

She glanced down at the simple ring, overwhelmed by the thought that he had purchased it all those years ago. Her heart practically sang aloud as she pondered the truth: *He has loved me all along. And I have loved him, too.* Nothing would ever change that.

Hand in hand, she and Chris eased their way through the crowd of people—many still clapping—and worked their way to the lobby. There, Dani met them, hands clasped together at her chest and a look of glee on her face.

"Congratulations!"

A chuckle rose up from the back of Adrianne's throat. "How did you hear?"

"Are you kidding?" Dani reached for Adrianne's hand to look at the ring. "Good news travels fast around here. I've practically got the wedding cake ordered. And I assume I'll be a bridesmaid."

"Correct assumption." Adrianne giggled.

"We're planning a wedding!" Dani spoke aloud, catching the eye and ear of a man passing by. When he gave her a curious look, she added, "For this happy couple." She pointed to them.

"Happy couple." We are a happy couple. And we're about to be a family, a real family.

With Chris's arm wrapped around her waist, Adrianne contemplated the great joy that threatened to overwhelm her. *Oh Lord, I'm so grateful. So very grateful.*

After finishing up her conversation with Dani, Adrianne went off in search of her boss, to ask for permission to leave early. *I came in late, and I'm leaving early. Hope he doesn't kill me.* Thankfully, she found Mr. Martinson in a good humor. He looked up as she entered his office.

"Hey," she started.

"Hey, back," he said. "I see you created quite a stir back in the Revolutionary War area."

"Oh, I'm sorry," she explained, "I. . . Good grief. How in the world did you hear so quickly?"

"Didn't hear. I saw it. With my own eyes."

"W–what?"

He grinned. "Security cameras. Recorded the whole thing."

Adrianne slapped herself in the head. "Oh no! I forgot about that."

"Yep. From the second the curtain dropped. Not a bad piece of film, let me tell you." He let out a laugh. "I've watched it twice already. Great stuff. Has all the elements of a great movie scene. Just let me know if you ever want a copy for your children."

She shook her head and dropped into a chair opposite him. "This is so embarrassing. A–are you upset?"

"Are you kidding? I think it's great. And great for business, too. Maybe the papers will pick up the story." His smile lit the room. "And besides, it's about time someone snagged you. I'm just glad it wasn't that Kenner fellow."

A wave of relief swept over her. "I'm so glad to hear you say that. I hope this doesn't hamper his contributions. He's been such an asset to the museum."

"Nah. He won't stop giving. He's been a staunch supporter for years." Bob looked up with a smile. "I think he had designs on you."

"Sorry about that. He's—"

"A guy with too much money to spend and too much time on his hands. You now. . ." He rose from his chair and came to stand beside her. "You deserve much more than that. I just hope this fellow you're marrying is worthy of you."

"Oh, he is." The warmth rose to her cheeks. "He's the best thing that ever happened to me, Mr. Martinson. He's a good man. Perfect for me in every way."

"A good fit, huh?"

"Yes." She smiled, thinking of Lorelei's words. "A perfect fit."

Mr. Martinson gave her a fatherly pat on the back. "Well, you're a great mom, and I know you're going to be a great wife."

"Thank you so much," she said. "That means a lot coming from you."

"You're welcome. Now, get out of here. I'm sure you have things to do, people to tell."

"I do." She turned, and with a wave sprinted back to the lobby, where she practically ran into Chris. Ironically, she found him chatting with Joey. *Ouch. This might be tricky.*

Joey looked her way with a shrug. "Hey."

"Hey."

"I, uh, I hear congratulations are in order." He stuck out his hand for a stilted handshake. "Congrats."

"Thanks."

"You're getting a great girl." Joey's words were meant for Chris, but his eyes never left Adrianne's.

"Thank you." Chris reached to slip his arm around Adrianne's shoulders. "I've been in love with this woman for as long as I can remember."

"I understand." Joey gave a curt nod, then turned back to his work.

"Don't worry about him," Dani leaned over to whisper in Adrianne's ear. "I have it on good authority he has a crush on at least three other female employees. His heart will mend."

"Yes, it will. I know the power of a mended heart, for sure. But thanks for telling me that. It helps."

"Something I need to know about?" Chris looked at her, curiosity in his eyes.

"Nah. I just think he was in love with me, is all."

"Ah. I see." He wrapped her in his arms and kissed her on

the forehead. "Well, I can't blame him for that, but he's going to have to fight me to get you. And he won't win, I'll promise you that. I almost lost you once. I'm not going to let that happen again."

"This guy is a keeper, Adrianne," Dani said with a sigh. "He's a prince of a guy if I ever saw one."

"What did you say?" She looked over at her friend, stunned.

Dani shrugged. "I just said that he was a prince. You know, if the shoe fits—"

"I know, I know." Adrianne giggled. "I guess it's unanimous, then." She slipped her hand into Chris's and together they headed off to tell Lorelei the good news.

twenty-two

Chris pulled out onto the turnpike in the direction of Adrianne's parents' house. He couldn't have stopped smiling if he'd tried. The joy that flooded over him was almost more than he could stand. Several times along the way, he unclasped his right hand from the steering wheel and reached to grab Adrianne's. How perfect it felt, wrapped in his. How right.

"What will we tell Lorelei?" he asked as he kissed the ends of Adrianne's fingertips.

She gave a little shrug. "Let's just see what happens in the moment, okay? No rehearsed speeches. I have an idea God is going to take it from here."

"I'd say He already has."

For the next several minutes, as they made their way along in the traffic, Chris laid out his plan for moving to Philadelphia. "I can still work with the missions organization," he said. "I'll do short-term jaunts, several a year, staying only a couple of weeks each time. And I'll find something to fill the gap on this end, I feel sure of it."

"Funny," she said with a childish grin. "That's just what Jake said."

"Really?"

She went on to tell him about the conversation she'd had with Jake and Katelyn just a few short days ago—how her beloved pastor planned to offer Chris a position at the church.

Chris responded with "Are you serious?" Then he went on to share more from his side. He told her the story of Brent and his wife, of their desire to settle into his home, and his position, in Nicaragua. When he finished, Adrianne looked over at him and simply shook her head, clearly too overcome to respond.

Chris pulled off of the turnpike in the direction of her parents' house. *No. My future in-laws' house.* There, he would lift Lorelei into his arms and hold on to her.

Forever.

&

Adrianne's heart sang as they approached her parents' house. She could hardly wait to see Lorelei, or rather, for Lorelei to see that Chris had come for them. As they started to get out of the car, Chris took her by the hand and lifted up a heartfelt prayer, for the Lord to guide every action, every word. Then he planted half a dozen tiny kisses on her cheek. "Ready?"

"Mm-hmm."

When they arrived at the front door, Adrianne motioned for Chris to give her a moment inside alone. He nodded in understanding. She opened the front door, surprised to find her mother in the living room alone, reading a book.

"Mom?"

Her mother looked up, surprised. "Oh, I was so engrossed in my story, I didn't even hear you come in." She glanced up at the wall clock. "You're early."

"I know." Adrianne giggled. "There's a reason for that." She cracked the door open a bit and motioned for Chris to come inside. As soon as he did, her mother sprang from the couch with a squeal.

"I knew it! I just knew it." The book dropped from her hand on to the sofa, and she crossed the room to wrap Chris in a motherly embrace.

"Mom?" Adrianne's heart swelled as she lifted her left hand for her mother to see the ring.

"O–oh, oh!" This time her mother captured them both with outstretched arms. "I'm the happiest woman on the planet."

"That might be debatable," Adrianne said with a wink. "I think maybe I've got you beat."

After a few more words of congratulations, they turned their attention to the most important thing.

"Where is Lorelei?" Chris asked.

"She's in the backyard with her grandpa. He's raking leaves."

"Let's surprise her," Adrianne suggested. She looked over at Chris. Nerves had clearly gotten the better of him. "It's going to be fine," she whispered.

He nodded, and they made their way to the back door. She led the way outside, surprised to find her father, rake in hand, but no daughter in sight.

"Dad?"

He turned to face her, a smile erupting the moment he saw Chris standing beside her. He came at once to join them, a teddy-bear hug nearly squeezing the life out of both of them. "This is a happy day, a happy day."

Another minute or two of explanation and congratulations passed before Adrianne voiced the question on her heart. "Dad, where's Lorelei?" She looked around, growing a bit nervous.

"Ah." He put a finger to his lips and pointed to a tall mound of leaves. *She's in there,* he mouthed. Then he whispered, "I think she's trying to hide from me, so I've been playing along."

"Ah-ha."

Adrianne and Chris eased their way across the yard to the heaping pile of autumn leaves. Just as they drew close, a lyrical sound ribboned through the leaves, catching everyone by surprise. The leaves fluttered a bit, and Lorelei's childlike voice rang out, "Someday my prince will come."

Adrianne clapped a hand over her mouth, hardly believing it. "Oh my."

"What's she singing?" Chris whispered.

"I, uh. . .I'm not sure you'd believe me."

His eyebrows elevated playfully as he whispered, "Try me."

She stifled a giggle, then leaned to speak softly into his ear. "Well, it's sort of a. . .well. . .a fairy-tale kind of thing."

"Fairy tale?" He shrugged. "Girl stuff?"

"Um. . .yeah."

Lorelei's song poured out from beneath the colorful mound of leaves, and suddenly Adrianne's breath caught in her throat as reality hit. She turned to glance at Chris, and the reminiscent look in his eyes told her right away that he understood the magnitude of what was happening right in front of them.

"Lorelei," he whispered.

Adrianne nodded, remembering the story, the reason for their daughter's name. Lorelei—the maiden along the Rhine River whose lyrical voice wooed sailors as their ships passed by.

For a moment, neither of them said anything. They leaned against each other, just listening as the song poured forth.

Adrianne stared at the red heap of leaves in blissful silence as another reality hit. *"Though they are red like crimson. . ."* The mound of brilliantly colored fall leaves now stood as a reminder of all God had done. *Red. Crimson.* Lorelei, their Lorelei, was encased on every side by the color red. Not a reminder of the sins of the past, but a clear and vivid picture of the forgiveness God had poured out on them all.

Just then, the youngster sprang up, her purple shirt and bright orange pants creating a fluorescent haze amid the leaves and shouted, "Gotcha!"

Lorelei's face was aglow with excitement—for a moment, anyway. The moment she laid eyes on Adrianne and Chris standing together, a look of confusion registered in her eyes, but for a moment. In a split second, she bounded from the leaves, shouting the word Adrianne had ached to hear her say for seven long years. . .

"Daddy!"

epilogue

"Can't you drive any faster?" Chris looked over at Stephen, who drove the streets of downtown Philly like a man possessed.

"I'm doing the best I can. There must be some kind of traffic jam ahead or something."

"I don't want to be late to my own wedding."

David, who had only arrived in Philadelphia an hour ago, chuckled from the back seat, then reached up and patted him on the shoulder. "You're plenty early. Calm down."

"I'm calm."

"Sure you are." David laughed loud and long.

"Remember what I told you the night before my wedding?" Stephen asked. When Chris shook his head, Stephen reminded him. "I said your wedding would be next. And I was right."

"Oh, that's right. You did." He remembered now. They'd been racing down a street on their way to Stephen and Julie's rehearsal dinner.

"If memory serves me right, you were worried about keeping Adrianne waiting that night," Stephen said with a grin.

"Kind of like today." Chris glanced down at his watch, his nerves a jumbled mess.

Stephen's expression changed all of a sudden. He gave Chris a pensive look. "Hey, I just thought of something."

"What?"

"That 'always a groomsman' thing. We won't be able to say that anymore."

"Yeah." Chris smiled. "I'm glad about that."

"It's going to be a great day," David said. "The best day of your life."

"I hope I can remember my vows. And you've got the ring, right?"

"Of course," Stephen said.

"And the limousine company, did you call them?"

"Called 'em." Stephen chuckled. "Deep breaths, my friend."

Suddenly, the church came into view. A feeling of comfort washed over Chris the moment he saw the building. "There it is. Right there." Over the past six months, Freedom Fellowship had become more than a home. It was a place he now loved—and served. "Not the prettiest church in town, but certainly a place where the Lord moves."

"Hey, it sure beats any of our buildings in Nicaragua," David said from the back seat. "Looks like a mansion to me."

"Just my kind of place," Stephen agreed.

Chris smiled at his buddies. It felt good, right, to have them here, with him on this special day. As they sprang from the car, he noticed a small box on the floor. "What's this?"

"I don't know, man. This is your car, remember?" Stephen laughed. "I was just the assigned driver for today. Something about the groom being too nervous—"

"Yeah. I know." Chris reached down to nab the box, and recognized it right away as Adrianne's. "Oh no. I've got to get this to her right away. I'll guarantee you the wedding won't go on unless I do."

"Must be pretty important," David said.

"Yep," Chris agreed. "More important than you might imagine."

❧

Adrianne looked up at her daughter and her bridesmaids with a smile. "What do you think of my hair?" she asked.

"It's amazing," Dani answered.

"Be-you-tee-ful!" Lorelei exclaimed.

Katelyn offered a reassuring smile. "I think you're going to be the prettiest bride I've ever seen. And I've seen a few."

"Thank you." Adrianne looked in the mirror once again, touching up her lipstick. "But I'm not going to look very pretty waltzing down the aisle in this old bathrobe. I think it's about time to put on my dress." She looked over at the beautiful gown, a duplicate of an eighteenth-century ball gown from the museum. A dress she had dreamed of wearing for years.

"Chris is going to flip when he sees you in this," Dani said.

"He flips *every* time he sees her," Lorelei said with a giggle. "Even when she's in jeans and a T-shirt, he still says she's the prettiest girl in the world."

Adrianne felt her cheeks flush. "You're embarrassing me. Besides, we need to stay focused. We don't need to be talking about all of that." She looked around the room, searching for a small, familiar box. "You're all dressed, and I've hardly started. H—have any of you seen my shoes?"

Dani looked up from the mirror, where she had been touching up her mascara. "Your what?"

"My shoes." A familiar frantic feeling gripped Adrianne as she scoped the room.

"Oh no!" Lorelei slapped herself in the head. "Not again, Mom."

"I know they're here," Adrianne said. "I remember distinctly. They were in the—" She racked her brain, trying to remember. "Oh, good grief. I think they were in the car. Chris's car. I meant to get them out last night after the rehearsal dinner."

"What?" Katelyn looked at her. "Are you sure? Want me to see if he's here yet?"

"Yeah, do you mind?"

At that moment, a knock on the door distracted them all.

Adrianne gripped her robe a bit tighter and motioned for the other ladies to get it.

"Who is it?" Dani asked through the door.

"Chris."

Adrianne shook her head and gave the women an imploring look. "We can't see each other today. Not before the wedding."

Chris's voice on the other side of the door distracted her for a moment. "I think I have something my beautiful bride might need."

"Oh, thank God." She almost went to the door without thinking, but Katelyn stopped her.

"I'll get them."

The door cracked open and Chris's hand appeared with a pair of delicate silver sandals dangling from his index finger. "Here you go, my lady. Your slippers."

"Mom!" Lorelei's eyes widened as she whispered, "He's got your shoes."

Adrianne put a hand to her heart and breathed a sigh of relief. "Thank goodness."

"No, Mom. Don't you get it? He's got your *shoes*." Her daughter stood with hands on her hips, clearly trying to make a point. "I *told* you he was Prince Charming."

She erupted into laughter and before they knew it, they were all giggling.

"Everything okay in there?" Chris asked, his hand still in view.

"F—fine." Adrianne signaled to shush her daughter.

Katelyn snatched the pumps from Chris's finger and sent him on his way with a quick "Thanks so much." She handed them to Adrianne, who slipped them on her feet right away.

"Time to get dressed." Katelyn now took on the role of wedding coordinator, snapping everyone to attention.

Adrianne's hands trembled as she reached for her dress.

"I've dreamed of this moment for years. I can hardly believe it's here."

"Believe it, Mom," Lorelei whispered.

"You deserve it, honey," Katelyn added.

Less than five minutes later, Adrianne stood fully dressed in the elaborate ball gown in front of the full-length mirror. She swished to the right and then the left, captivated by the way she felt wearing it.

"That beadwork is amazing," Katelyn said. "I've never seen anything like it."

"There hasn't been anything like it for over two hundred years," Dani said with a smile. "Trust me. It's patterned after a one-of-a-kind gown from the Revolutionary War era."

"Something old *and* something new, all in one gown." Katelyn said. "Gorgeous *and* practical."

"Yes," Adrianne said with a smile. "And I've borrowed this necklace from my mother." She fingered the beautiful piece that draped her neck. "It was my grandmother's."

"It's so pretty," Lorelei said.

"What about the 'something blue' part?" Katelyn asked.

"Right here!" Dani held up the baby blue garter, trimmed in lace.

"Ooh, I almost forgot that." Adrianne quickly slipped it on.

"Almost done. Just one more thing." Dani reached up to fasten the delicate veil into Adrianne's hair, then placed a beautiful tiara on top. When she was finished, they all stood in silence a moment, just staring.

"Oh, Mom!" Lorelei stared at both of their reflections in the mirror. "You look like Cinderella."

"Do I?"

Katelyn and Dani nodded.

"You look like a queen," Lorelei whispered, her eyes wide.

Adrianne gazed down into her daughter's beautiful eyes. "If

I'm a queen," she said, "then that would make you a princess."

"Ooh. That's true." Lorelei turned to look at herself in the mirror once again. "I'm a princess."

An abrupt knock on the door interrupted their ponderings.

"It's almost time, honey," Adrianne's mother's voice rang out. "Is it okay if Daddy and I come in?"

"Yes. Of course."

Her parents entered the room and she turned to greet them. Her father's eyes filled at once. "You look beautiful," he whispered. "Absolutely beautiful." He reached up to kiss her on the cheek.

Her mother reached into her purse for a tissue. "I told myself I wouldn't cry today."

"It's okay, Mom." She grabbed her mother's hand and gave it a squeeze. "I'm sure by the time this day is over we'll all be drying our eyes."

Katelyn, still playing the role of organizer, handed each woman a bouquet to carry. From outside the door, the familiar strains of "Trumpet Voluntaire" rang out.

"I think that's our cue." Adrianne's father extended his arm. "Are you ready?"

She took it with a smile. "I'm ready."

With her bridesmaids and daughter leading the way, they made their way down the hallway toward the back of the sanctuary. The doors swept open, and for the first time, she saw her groom-to-be. He looked every bit like a prince in his black tuxedo and tails. His face glowed with excitement, and all the more when he finally caught a glimpse of her.

She watched as, one by one, her bridesmaids took their places at the front, and then, with great joy, as Lorelei made her way up the aisle, dropping rose petals all the way. *My little girl. My princess.* Something from the front distracted her. She looked up just in time to see Chris wipe his eyes as Lorelei went by. He mouthed a silent *I love you* to their daughter and she responded with a nod of her head.

As the wedding march began, Adrianne happened to glance down at her flowers. Most would have chosen pastels for a springtime wedding. *But not me.* No, nothing but red roses would do for a day like today.

"Though they are red like crimson. . ."

A wave of joy washed over her as she looked forward—into her bridegroom's eyes. She pushed back the lump in her throat as the Lord reminded her, once and for all, that the past truly *was* in the past.

With a prayer on her lips and a song in her heart, Adrianne took her first step down the aisle—toward her future.

A Letter To Our Readers

Dear Reader:
In order that we might better contribute to your reading enjoyment, we would appreciate your taking a few minutes to respond to the following questions. We welcome your comments and read each form and letter we receive. When completed, please return to the following:

Fiction Editor
Heartsong Presents
PO Box 719
Uhrichsville, Ohio 44683

1. Did you enjoy reading *Red Like Crimson* by Janice A. Thompson?
   ❑ Very much! I would like to see more books by this author!
   ❑ Moderately. I would have enjoyed it more if

   _____

   _____

   _____

2. Are you a member of **Heartsong Presents**?   ❑ Yes   ❑ No
   If no, where did you purchase this book? _____

   _____

3. How would you rate, on a scale from 1 (poor) to 5 (superior), the cover design? _____

4. On a scale from 1 (poor) to 10 (superior), please rate the following elements.

   ____ Heroine   ____ Plot
   ____ Hero   ____ Inspirational theme
   ____ Setting   ____ Secondary characters

5. These characters were special because? _____

_____

_____

6. How has this book inspired your life? _____

_____

_____

7. What settings would you like to see covered in future
   Heartsong Presents books? _____

_____

_____

8. What are some inspirational themes you would like to see
   treated in future books? _____

_____

_____

9. Would you be interested in reading other **Heartsong
   Presents** titles? ❏ Yes ❏ No

10. Please check your age range:
    ❏ Under 18   ❏ 18-24
    ❏ 25-34   ❏ 35-45
    ❏ 46-55   ❏ Over 55

Name _____

Occupation _____

Address _____

City, State, Zip _____

GONE
with the
GROOM

Annie Peterson, mother of the bride-to-be, works to solve the riddle of the missing fiancé in *Gone with the Groom*, a fun and riveting romance-mystery by Janice A. Thompson.

Contemporary, paperback, 304 pages, 5³⁄₁₆" x 8"

Please send me ____ copies of *Gone with the Groom*.
I am enclosing $9.97 for each.
(Please add $3.00 to cover postage and handling per order. OH add 7% tax.
If outside the U.S. please call 740-922-7280 for shipping charges.)

Name_____

Address _____

City, State, Zip _____

To place a credit card order, call 1-740-922-7280.
Send to: Heartsong Presents Readers' Service, PO Box 721, Uhrichsville, OH 44683

Hearts♥ng

CONTEMPORARY ROMANCE IS CHEAPER BY THE DOZEN!

Any 12 Heartsong Presents titles for only $27.00*

Buy any assortment of twelve *Heartsong Presents* titles and save 25% off the already discounted price of $2.97 each!

*plus $3.00 shipping and handling per order and sales tax where applicable. If outside the U.S. please call 740-922-7280 for shipping charges.

HEARTSONG PRESENTS TITLES AVAILABLE NOW:

___HP497 *Flames of Deceit*, R. Dow & A. Snaden
___HP498 *Charade*, P. Humphrey
___HP501 *The Thrill of the Hunt*, T. H. Murray
___HP502 *Whole in One*, A. Ford
___HP505 *Happily Ever After*, M. Panagiotopoulos
___HP506 *Cords of Love*, L. A. Coleman
___HP509 *His Christmas Angel*, G. Sattler
___HP510 *Past the Ps Please*, Y. Lehman
___HP513 *Licorice Kisses*, D. Mills
___HP514 *Roger's Return*, M. Davis
___HP517 *The Neighborly Thing to Do*, W. E. Brunstetter
___HP518 *For a Father's Love*, J. A. Grote
___HP521 *Be My Valentine*, J. Livingston
___HP522 *Angel's Roost*, J. Spaeth
___HP525 *Game of Pretend*, J. Odell
___HP526 *In Search of Love*, C. Lynxwiler
___HP529 *Major League Dad*, K. Y'Barbo
___HP530 *Joe's Diner*, G. Sattler
___HP533 *On a Clear Day*, Y. Lehman
___HP534 *Term of Love*, M. Pittman Crane
___HP537 *Close Enough to Perfect*, T. Fowler
___HP538 *A Storybook Finish*, L. Bliss
___HP541 *The Summer Girl*, A. Boeshaar
___HP542 *Clowning Around*, W. E. Brunstetter
___HP545 *Love Is Patient*, C. M. Hake
___HP546 *Love Is Kind*, J. Livingston
___HP549 *Patchwork and Politics*, C. Lynxwiler
___HP550 *Woodhaven Acres*, B. Etchison
___HP553 *Bay Island*, B. Loughner
___HP554 *A Donut a Day*, G. Sattler
___HP557 *If You Please*, T. Davis
___HP558 *A Fairy Tale Romance*, M. Panagiotopoulos
___HP561 *Ton's Vow*, K. Cornelius
___HP562 *Family Ties*, J. L. Barton
___HP565 *An Unbreakable Hope*, K. Billerbeck
___HP566 *The Baby Quilt*, J. Livingston

___HP569 *Ageless Love*, L. Bliss
___HP570 *Beguiling Masquerade*, C. G. Page
___HP573 *In a Land Far Far Away*, M. Panagiotopoulos
___HP574 *Lambert's Pride*, L. A. Coleman and R. Hauck
___HP577 *Anita's Fortune*, K. Cornelius
___HP578 *The Birthday Wish*, J. Livingston
___HP581 *Love Online*, K. Billerbeck
___HP582 *The Long Ride Home*, A. Boeshaar
___HP585 *Compassion's Charm*, D. Mills
___HP586 *A Single Rose*, P. Griffin
___HP589 *Changing Seasons*, C. Reece and J. Reece-Demarco
___HP590 *Secret Admirer*, G. Sattler
___HP593 *Angel Incognito*, J. Thompson
___HP594 *Out on a Limb*, G. Gaymer Martin
___HP597 *Let My Heart Go*, B. Huston
___HP598 *More Than Friends*, T. H. Murray
___HP601 *Timing is Everything*, T. V. Bateman
___HP602 *Dandelion Bride*, J. Livingston
___HP605 *Picture Imperfect*, N. J. Farrier
___HP606 *Mary's Choice*, Kay Cornelius
___HP609 *Through the Fire*, C. Lynxwiler
___HP610 *Going Home*, W. E. Brunstetter
___HP613 *Chorus of One*, J. Thompson
___HP614 *Forever in My Heart*, L. Ford
___HP617 *Run Fast, My Love*, P. Griffin
___HP618 *One Last Christmas*, J. Livingston
___HP621 *Forever Friends*, T. H. Murray
___HP622 *Time Will Tell*, L. Bliss
___HP625 *Love's Image*, D. Mayne
___HP626 *Down From the Cross*, J. Livingston
___HP629 *Look to the Heart*, T. Fowler
___HP630 *The Flat Marriage Fix*, K. Hayse
___HP633 *Longing for Home*, C. Lynxwiler
___HP634 *The Child Is Mine*, M. Colvin
___HP637 *Mother's Day*, J. Livingston
___HP638 *Real Treasure*, T. Davis

(If ordering from this page, please remember to include it with the order form.)